Motherly
Devotion

To *My Mother with*
lots of Love

From _____

Lillie Petronella

+Klaas

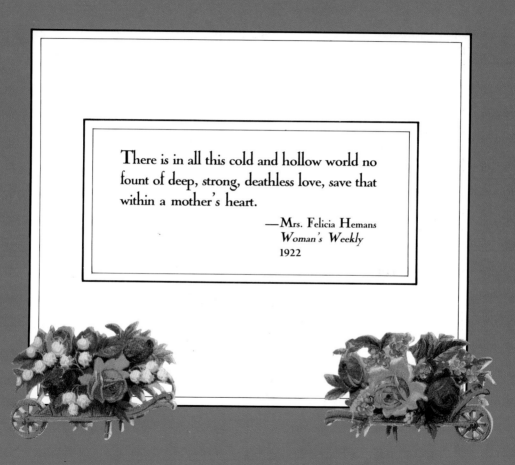

There is in all this cold and hollow world no fount of deep, strong, deathless love, save that within a mother's heart.

—Mrs. Felicia Hemans
Woman's Weekly
1922

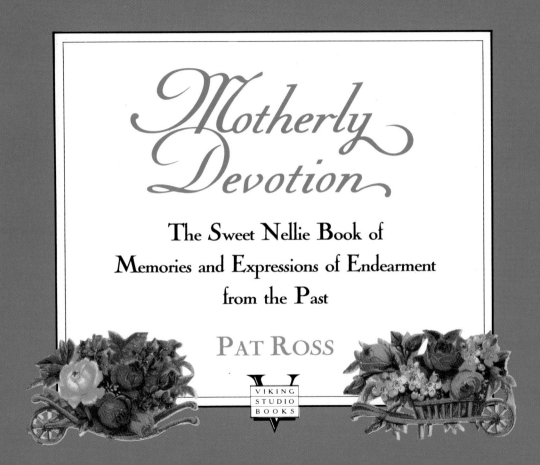

Motherly Devotion

The Sweet Nellie Book of
Memories and Expressions of Endearment
from the Past

PAT ROSS

VIKING
STUDIO
BOOKS

VIKING STUDIO BOOKS
Published by the Penguin Group
Viking Penguin, a division of Penguin Books USA Inc.,
375 Hudson Street, New York, New York 10014, U.S.A.
Penguin Books Ltd, 27 Wrights Lane, London W8 5TZ, England
Penguin Books Australia Ltd, Ringwood, Victoria, Australia
Penguin Books Canada Ltd, 2801 John Street, Markham, Ontario, Canada L3R 1B4
Penguin Books (N.Z.) Ltd, 182–190 Wairau Road, Auckland 10, New Zealand

Penguin Books Ltd, Registered Offices: Harmondsworth, Middlesex, England

First published in 1990 by Viking Penguin, a division of Penguin Books USA Inc.

5   7   9   10   8   6   4

Copyright © Pat Ross, 1990
All rights reserved

LIBRARY OF CONGRESS CATALOGING-IN-PUBLICATION DATA
Motherly devotion : the Sweet Nellie book of memories and expressions
of endearment from the past / [compiled by] Pat Ross.
p.   cm.
ISBN 0-670-83059-3
1. Mothers—Quotations, maxims, etc.   I. Ross, Pat. 1943–
PN6084.M6M665   1990
082'.085'2—dc20   89-40651

Printed in Japan   Set in Nicholas Cochin
Designed by Amy Hill

AN APPRECIATION

It seems appropriate somehow that the first person on my list to thank is my mother, Anita Kienzle, for her enthusiastic and tireless research for this book in her hometown of Baltimore. Her missives were always jammed with copious notes, clippings, and humorous remarks that kept me going. She wishes to acknowledge the libraries in her area, especially the Enoch Pratt Free Library and the Maryland Historical Society Library, for their guidance and special reference materials. To keep things in the family, I relied on my grandmother's etiquette and entertainment books, which now grace my own shelves at home.

Leisa Crane, who has been a steady partner during the preparation of my "mini-manners" books, brings taste, wit, and style to her indefatigable research. My thanks also to Olivia Serafini-Sauli for adding a youthful perspective to the research.

These small books are deceptive in their size, for they require the assistance and devotion of many to make them perfect. For their help in finding the most expressive illustrative material, my appreciation goes to Sven and Susan

Miller, Mary Santangelo, and Bonnie Ferris. And, by now, the list of libraries, librarians, and historical societies has grown too enormous to mention individually by name.

The usual support staff is always on my mind when it comes to thanks: the staff at Sweet Nellie, the many people at Viking—most especially Michael Fragnito, Barbara Williams, Amy Hill, and Michael Kaye—and, of course, Amy Berkower, Sheila Callahan, and Mabel Cramm are always there for me at Writers House.

How many times can I thank my husband, Joel, and daughter, Erica? Not enough, that is certain!

INTRODUCTION

Singing the praises of mothers and motherhood is a centuries-old tradition. The ancient Greeks celebrated with a spring fête that they dedicated to Rhea, queen of the Titans. The fourth Sunday in Lent was, for the early Christians, a time to honor Mary, Christ's mother. Eventually, that day became known as Mothering Sunday, a time to honor all mothers. In 1914, here in the United States, Congress passed a resolution to set aside the second Sunday in May as "a public expression of our love and reverence for the mothers of our country." A Pennsylvania schoolteacher, Anna M. Jarvis, is credited as the person who first began lobbying for a special day to memorialize mothers. For some seventy-five years now, mothers have been cherished in an official way on that well-loved Sunday.

The word "mother" evokes universal memories that have not changed with the passing of time: bedtime stories, the sweet smell of talcum, cool hands and warm drinks, dutiful scoldings over boots not worn and mittens lost, and, yes, corny as it sounds, Mom's apple pie. For today's modern mother, such a list might also include the sound of the car warming up for yet another trip to the athletic field; a late-afternoon phone call from the office to inquire about the big math exam; and skill and patience for fixing bikes and anything battery operated. Too often we slip up on the thank-yous and everyday gratitude. It's fortunate that Mother's Day helps us to remember.

How well I recall rising early every Mother's Day, waking my younger sister, and tiptoeing down the stairs to the kitchen. We whispered "Hush!" and "Quiet!" in the silence, trying hard not to rattle the pots and pans as we went about preparing an elaborate breakfast tray for Mother. Year after year, we cried "Surprise!" when we brought the tray to her bedside, and, always, she seemed genuinely surprised and delighted. One year I made earrings for her from my shell kit. The earrings contained far more dried epoxy than shells, but Mother proudly wore them to church that morning. As a mother now myself, I have cherished my own daughter's colorful weavings made especially for me at camp and the small clay pot she made to resemble my shop, complete with a door and tiny sign that says SWEET NELLIE.

The affection felt over the years for mothers, grandmothers, aunts, and other special women in our lives has found its way into words on many printed pages in countless forms. The nineteenth and early twentieth century saw a flowering of poems, songs, and other published remembrances that are perfect for this book. The heartfelt sentiments expressed in letters and diaries of the time—written by women and men—add even more personal thoughts and insights. *Motherly Devotion* brings together this small but special selection of pieces from an era that still speaks to us today, and helps us to celebrate the special place that mothers hold in our hearts.

Mother

Every Mother

There is no slave out of heaven like a loving woman; and, of all loving women, there is no such slave as a mother.

—Henry Ward Beecher
Proverbs from Plymouth Pulpit
1887

A mother-in-law has the name and repute
Of whims and of temper and a love for dispute;
She is roundly abused and maliciously slandered,
An innocent victim, most unjustly bantered.
This is all wrong, and defying objection,
I hold she's a woman of heart and affection.
So here's to the mother of our husband or wife—
God bless her and give her good health and long life!

—*Prosit: A Book of Toasts*
Compiled by Clotho
1904

OTHERING SUNDAY

It is the day of all the year,
Of all the year the one day,
And here come I, my Mother dear,
To bring you cheer,
A-mothering on Sunday.

—Anonymous

SUGGESTIONS FOR PLACE CARDS FOR A MOTHERING SUNDAY DINNER

God cannot be everywhere, so He made mothers.

—Arab proverb

A mother is a mother still,
The holiest thing alive.

—Samuel Taylor Coleridge
"The Three Graves"
1818

Her children arise up,
and call her blessed.

—Proverbs XXXI:28

Every beetle is a gazelle in the eyes of its mother.

—Moorish proverb

A rich child often sits in a poor mother's lap.

—Danish proverb

When I was six I made my mother a little hat—out of her new blouse.

—Lilly Dache
1954

NOBODY knows of the work it makes
To keep the home together,
Nobody knows of the steps it takes,
Nobody knows—but mother.

—Anonymous

If you've a mother with silv'ry hair,
Give her all pleasures and treat her with care.
And as you grow older the least you can do,
Is do unto mother as she did unto you.

— Verse from a nineteenth-century calling card

FROM A MOTHER'S JOURNAL

Nothing keeps the heart so fresh and young, saves it from bitterness and corrosion through the cares and conflicts and disappointments of life, as the daily enjoyment of a happy home. May I always keep this in remembrance, and do everything that lies in my power to make our home the happiest spot on earth for our children.

—Mrs. H. O. Ward
Sensible Etiquette of the Best Society
1878

The goodness of a home is not dependent on wealth, or spaciousness, or beauty, or luxury. Everything depends on the Mother.

—G. W. E. Russell
"More, Please"
1910

Wise Mothers

Judicious mothers will always keep in mind that they are the first book read, and the last put aside, in every child's library.

—C. Lenox Redmond
1926

The mother's heart is the child's school-room.

—Henry Ward Beecher
Proverbs from Plymouth Pulpit
1887

Almost all women have a passionate admiration for what is called genius, and nothing so delights a mother as to hear it asserted that her child is very uncommon, very unlike ordinary children.

—Jennie June
Talks on Women's Topics
1864

Education is the mental railway, beginning at birth, and running on to eternity. No hand can lay it in the right direction but the hand of a mother.

—Mrs. H. O. Ward
Sensible Etiquette of the Best Society
1878

A mother's love and prayers and tears are seldom lost on even the most wayward child.

—A. E. Davis
American Etiquette and Rules of Politeness
1882

Well may both preachers and mothers falter, and feel at times that they hardly know how to wait for the growth of the seed that they have planted. Fear not, watch the field, pull up the tares by the root, and if the seed has been good, and the soil is good, there will yet be an abundant harvest for those who remain to gather it.

—Mrs. H. O. Ward
Sensible Etiquette of the Best Society
1878

Upon the mother devolves the duty of planting in the hearts of her children those seeds of love and virtue which shall develop useful and happy lives. There are no words to express the relation of a mother to her children.

—A. E. Davis
American Etiquette and Rules of Politeness
1882

Thou art thy mother's glass, and she in thee
Calls back the lovely April of her prime.

—*Shakespeare*
Sonnet III
1609

Like one, like the other
Like daughter, like mother.

—Anonymous

In passing we may say that a girl is always safe
who gives a wise and loving mother her entire
confidence, and a mother is her child's very best
counselor and chaperone.

—Margaret E. Sangster
Good Manners for All Occasions
1904

**M**y Dear Mary,

How lonely the house seems—I never knew before how well you helped to fill it. I am anxious to hear of your first impressions of the city and how you like your new home. Ever since you went away, I have been wondering if it was as hard for you to go out into the world as it was for me to have you go.

Don't write short, hurried letters, simply stating facts in their tersest form, but tell me all your thoughts and dreams and plans, your worries and trials, and we will talk them over as two comrades. . . . If there is anything in my life that can be of value to you, I want you to have it; if I can save you a stumble or a single false step, I want to do it, but the only way I can do it is to know your heart.

Your loving mother

—Florence Wenderoth Saunders
Letters to a Business Girl
1908

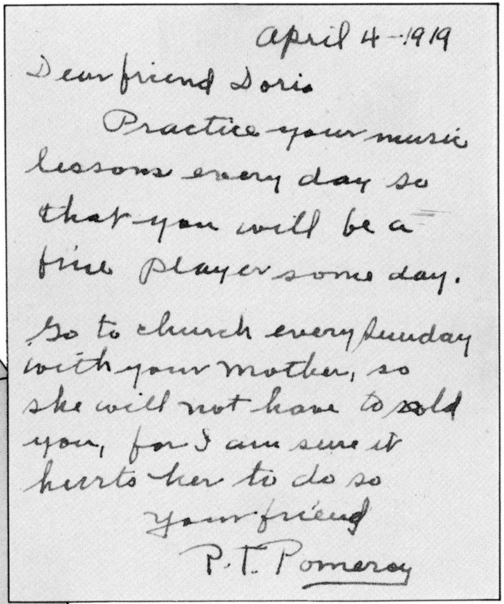

april 4 – 1919

Dear friend Doris

Practice your music
lessons every day so
that you will be a
fine player some day.

Go to church every Sunday
with your mother, so
she will not have to scold
you, for I am sure it
hurts her to do so
Your friend
P. T. Pomeroy

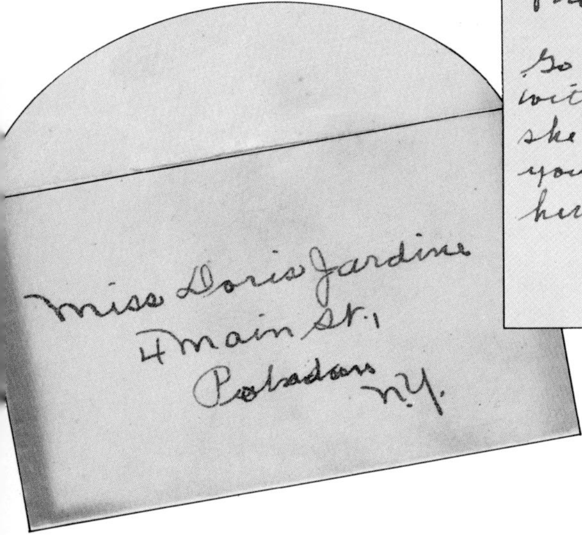

Miss Doris Jardine
4 Main St,
Potsdam
N.Y.

They always looked back before turning the corner, for their mother was always at the window to nod and smile, and wave her hand at them. Somehow it seemed as if they couldn't have got through the day without that, for whatever their mood might be, the last glimpse of that motherly face was sure to affect them like sunshine.

—Louisa May Alcott
Little Women
1868

Mothers and Sons

Children are what mothers are;
No fondest father's fondest care
Can fashion so the infant's heart
As those creative beams that dart,
With all their hopes and fears, upon
The cradle of a sleeping son.
—Walter Savage Landor
1775–1864

Begin, little boy, to recognize your mother with a smile.

—Virgil
Eclogues, II
37 B.C.

The years, as they come, every one, deepen my gratitude to you, as I better understand the significance of life, and every one adds to the affection that never was small. God bless you.

—Letter from Walter Hines Page to his mother
December 21, 1893

Who is it that loves me and will love me
for ever with an affection which no chance,
no misery, no crime of mine can do away?—
It is you, my mother.

—Letter from Thomas Carlyle to his mother
August 29, 1824

In the Heavens above,
The angels, whispering to one another,
Can find, among their burning terms of love,
None so devotional as that of
"Mother."

—Edgar Allan Poe
"To My Mother"
1845

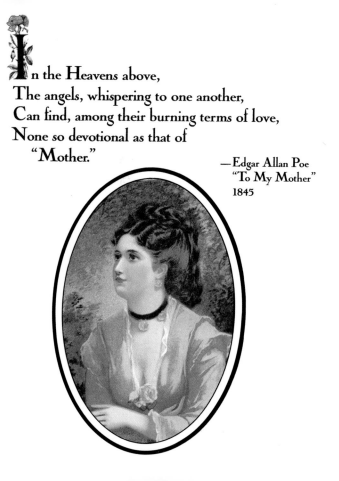

Let France have good mothers,
and she will have good sons.

—Napoleon

New Mothers

Today, at 12 minutes past 1 o'clock p.m. my precious, wee girlie came to her mother. . . . The dearest, sweetest, little treasure ever a mother had. . . . As soon as she was all here, all suffering ceased and I feel as strong as an ox.

—From the diary of Martha Shaw
1893

What is the reason of the singular passion which mothers seem to have for enormous babies? From the delight and triumph with which a ten-pound baby is exhibited, one would imagine that babies, like Chinese wives, were valued according to their weight.

—Jennie June
Talks on Women's Topics
1864

Over my slumbers your loving watch keep;—
Rock me to sleep, mother,—rock me to sleep!

—Elizabeth Akers Allen
"Rock Me to Sleep"
1860

The hand that rocks
The cradle
Is the hand that rules
The world.

—W. R. Wallace
"The Hand that Rules
The World"
1865

NESTLING TIME

Nestling closely, while kisses sweet
Fall on the dainty hands and feet,
As Mother is making all ready for bed
And slumber, her wee little "sleepy head."

Oh, nestling hour, so sweet, so blest,
When comes my birdling to her nest!
How we love it, my baby and I,
As we sing in the starshine our "lullaby."

—Mary D. Brice
1901

 # BABY SKIES

Would you know the baby skies?
Baby's skies are mother's eyes.
Mother's eyes and smile together
Make the baby's pleasant weather.

Mother, keep your eyes from tears,
Keep your heart from foolish fears,
Keep your lips from dull complaining
Lest the baby think 'tis raining.

—Mary C. Bartlett
1900

TO MY MOTHER

You too, my mother, read my rhymes
For love of unforgotten times,
And you may chance to hear once more
The little feet along the floor.

—Robert Louis Stevenson
A Child's Garden of Verses
1905

Women know
The way to rear up children (to be just)
They know a simple, merry, tender knack
Of tying sashes, fitting baby-shoes,
And stringing pretty words that make no sense,
And kissing full sense into empty words.

—Elizabeth Barrett Browning
"Motherless"
1856

It seems fitting that a book about traditions of the past should be decorated with period artwork. In that spirit, the art in *Motherly Devotion* has been taken from personal collections of original nineteenth- and early twentieth-century calling cards, drawings, and popular paper treasures of the time.

The endpapers and chapter openings contain patterns reproduced from some of our favorite vintage wallpapers.

Mama.

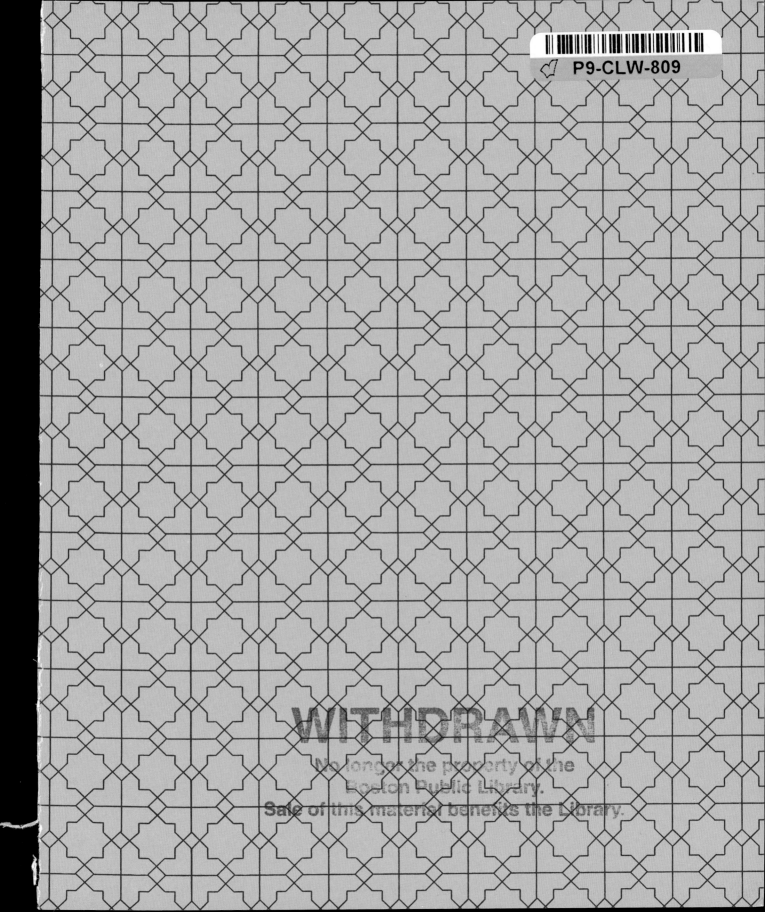

Sabrina

BY NICK DRNASO
DRAWN & QUARTERLY

DRAWNANDQUARTERLY.COM

FIRST EDITION: MAY 2018
SECOND PRINTING: OCTOBER 2018
THIRD PRINTING: SEPTEMBER 2018
FOURTH PRINTING: SEPTEMBER 2018
FIFTH PRINTING: NOVEMBER 2018

PRINTED IN CHINA

10 9 8 7 6 5

CATALOGING DATA AVAILABLE FROM
LIBRARY AND ARCHIVES CANADA.

PUBLISHED IN THE USA BY DRAWN & QUARTERLY,
A CLIENT PUBLISHER OF FARRAR, STRAUS AND GIROUX.
ORDERS: 888-330-8477

PUBLISHED IN CANADA BY DRAWN & QUARTERLY,
A CLIENT PUBLISHER OF RAINCOAST BOOKS.
ORDERS: 800-663-5714

THANKS: KYLE HORTON, IVAN BRUNETTI, TRACY HURREN, CHRIS OLIVEROS,
CHRISTEN CARTER, MICHELLE OLLIE, HARRY BLISS, JAMES STURM, SUSAN O'DELL,
ZADIE SMITH, TONY TULATHIMUTTE, ADRIAN TOMINE, JONATHAN LETHEM,
CHRIS WARE, PEGGY BURNS, TOM DEVLIN, JULIA POHL-MIRANDA, RACHEL NAM.

♥ FOR SARAH. ♥

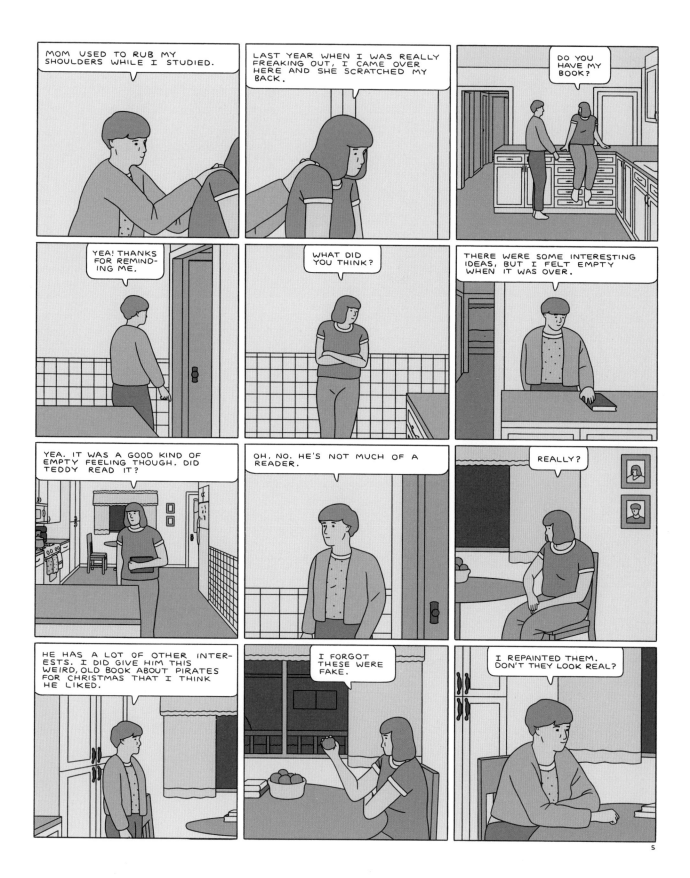

9

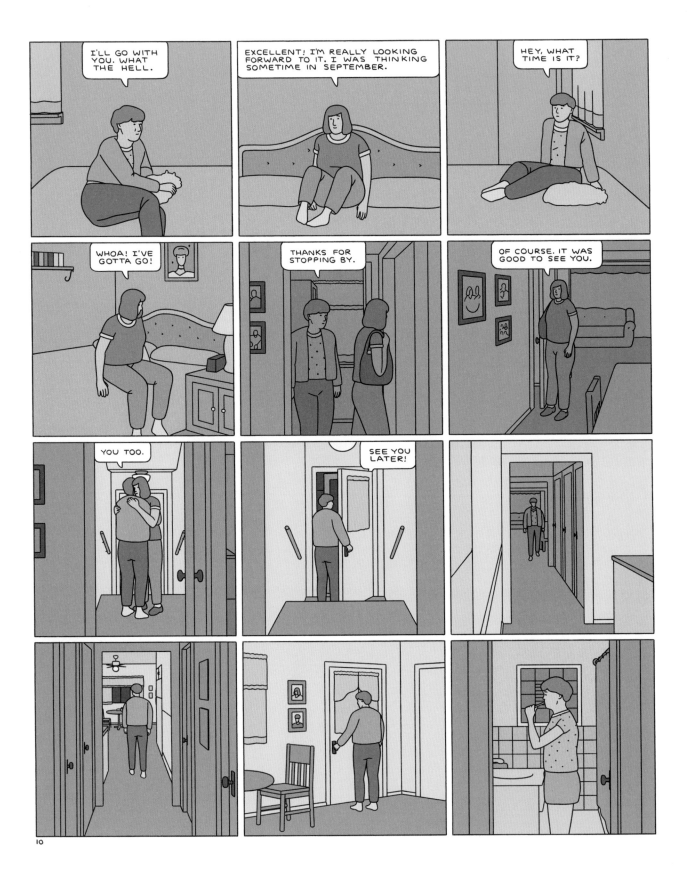

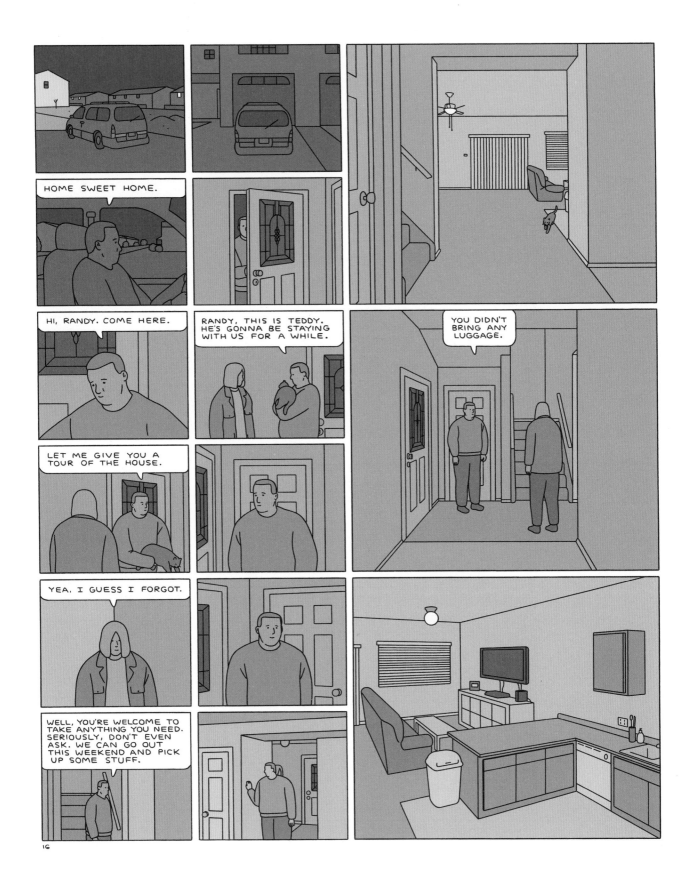

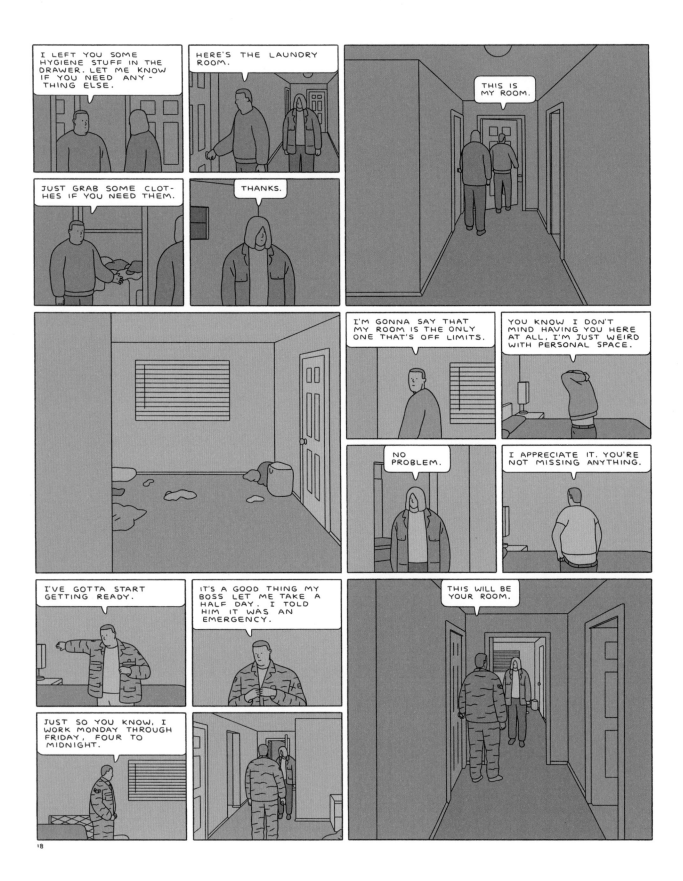

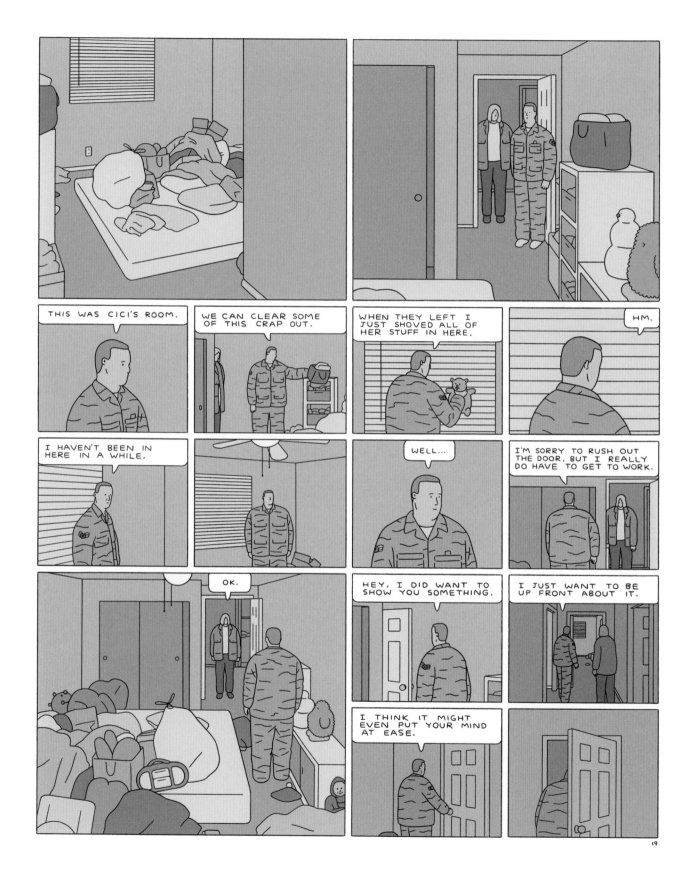

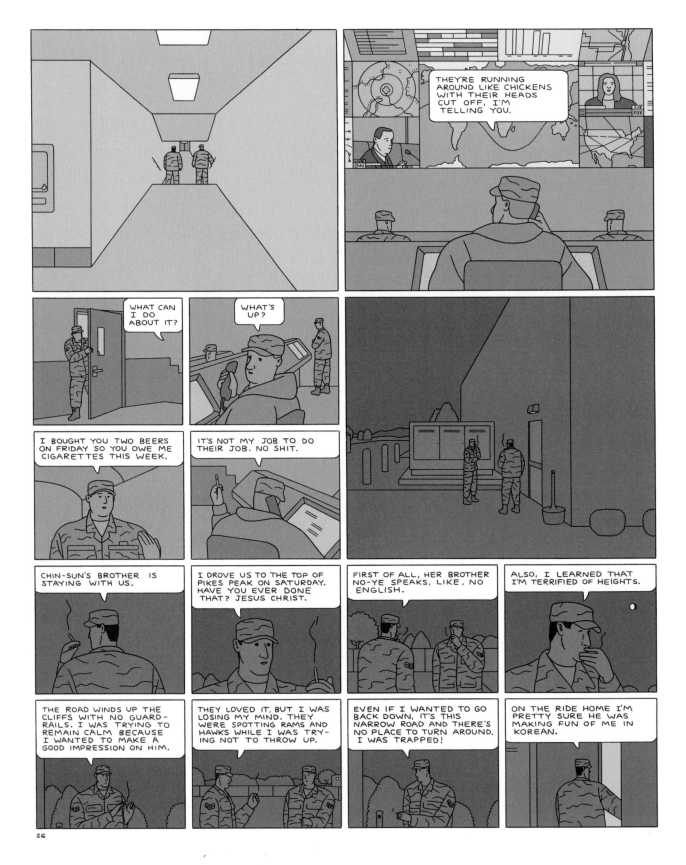

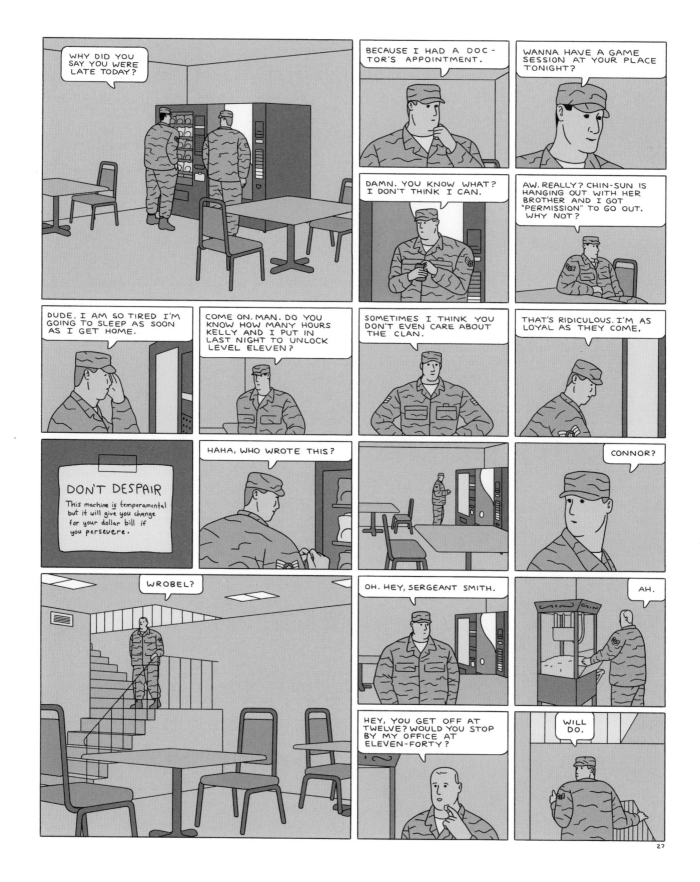

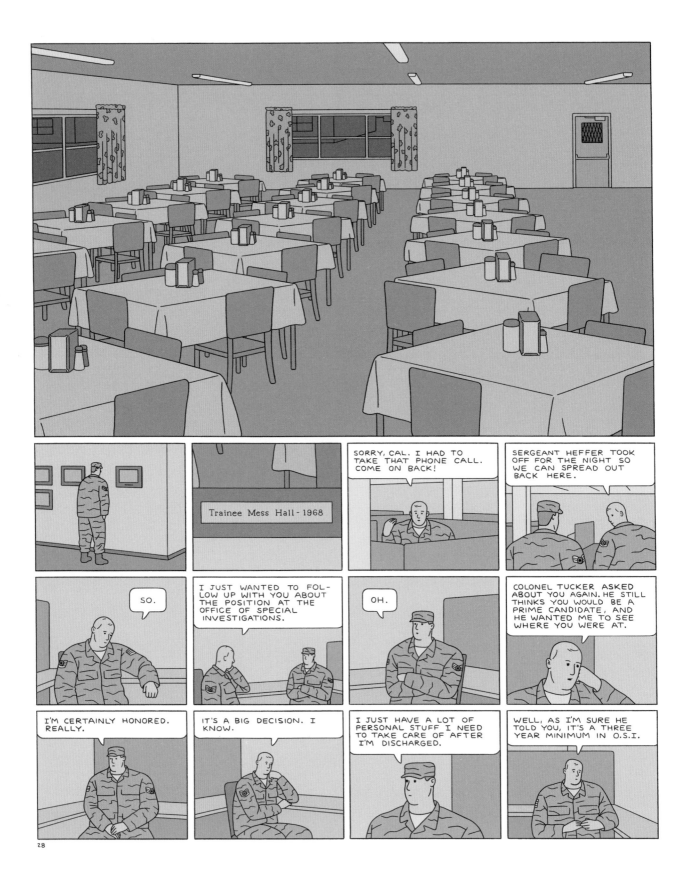

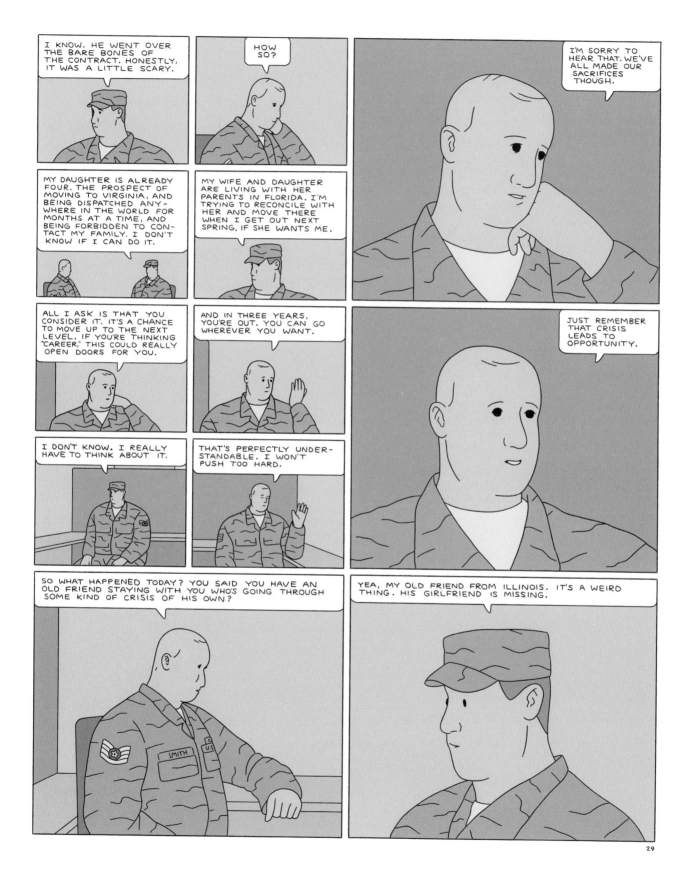

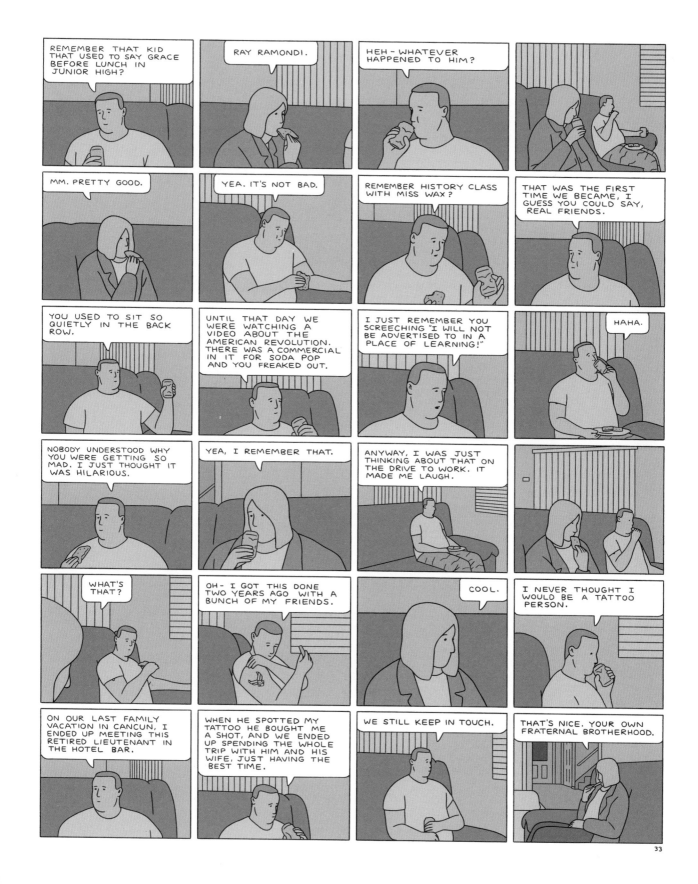

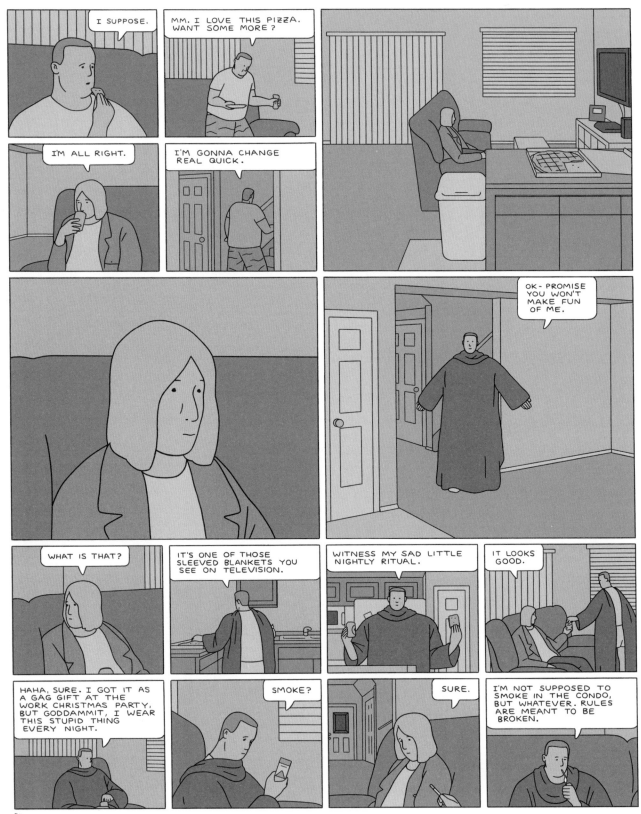

>> Inside the memorial museum, we travel seven stories below street level, right down to the bedrock on which the Twin Towers once stood.

>> A tour of the museum is a virtual history of vivid sights and sounds designed to transport visitors back to that day.

>> Viewers relive the tragedy in painful detail through 23000 pictures and over 10000 artifacts, creating an overwhelmingly visceral sensation.

NO DAY SHALL ERASE YOU ...SE YOU FROM THE MEMORY OF TIME
Virgil

>> Behind this wall is a repository housing some 8000 unidentified human remains.

>> My sister died on Flight 1-7-5. The grief stays with me every day.

>> Our goal is to pay tribute to the ones that were lost that day. The heroes, the first responders, the innocent victims.

>> We want guests to leave with an increased sense of the value of a human life, that each one is important and won't be forgotten.

>> It was an event that changed life as we know it forever. It's our duty to preserve that moment for people a hundred years from now.

>> This is a sacred place. A part of history.

>> After touring the museum, I definitely have a greater appreciation for the sacrifices that were made here.

>> Like every American, I have a lot of personal memories wrapped up in 9-1-1. It is important to look back and reflect on how far we've come.

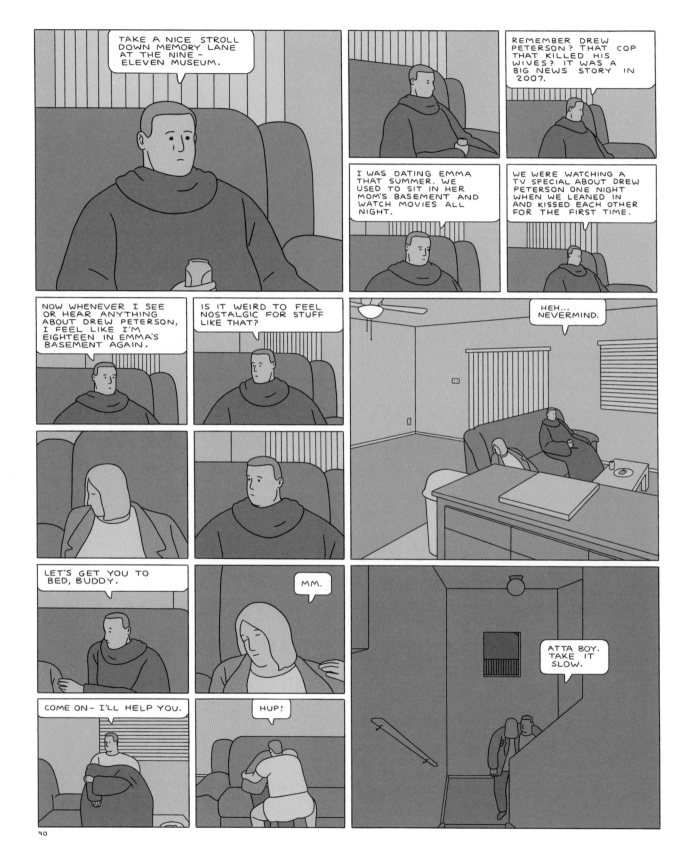

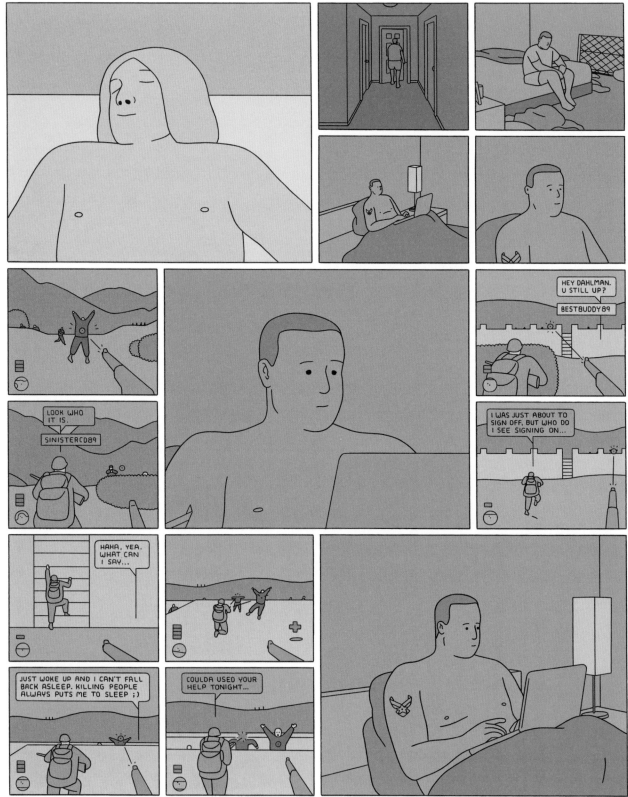

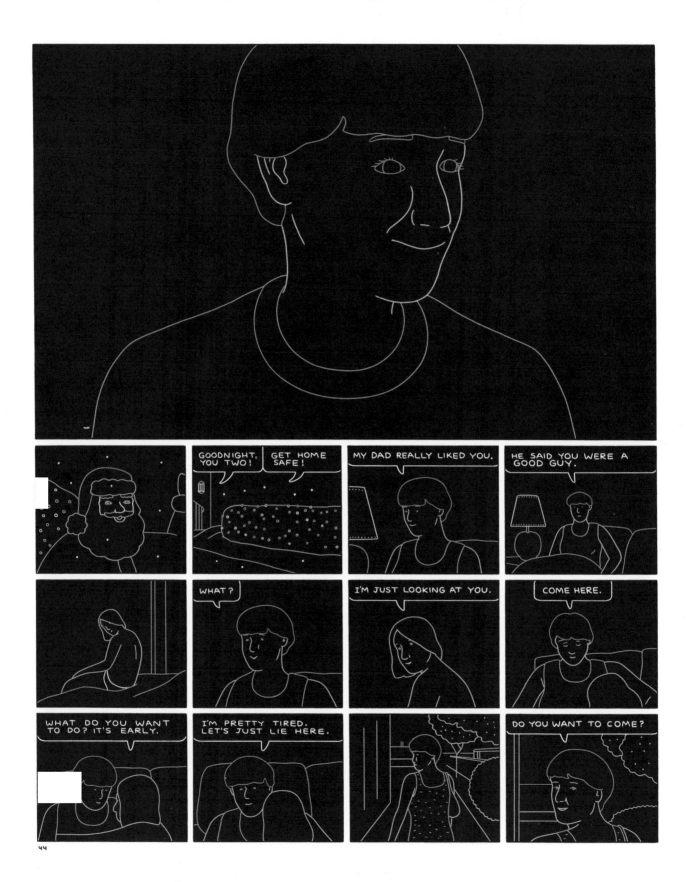

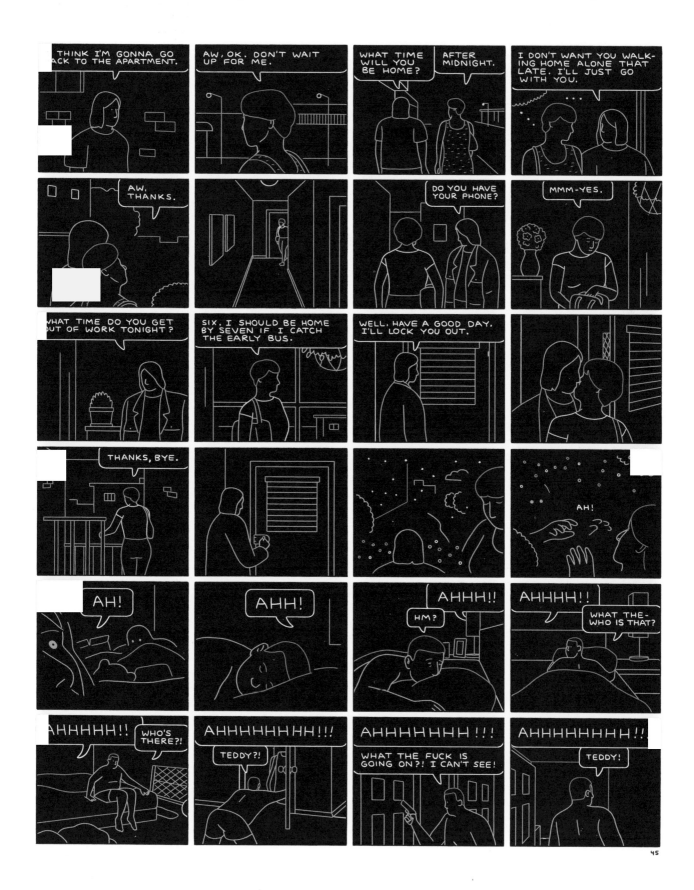

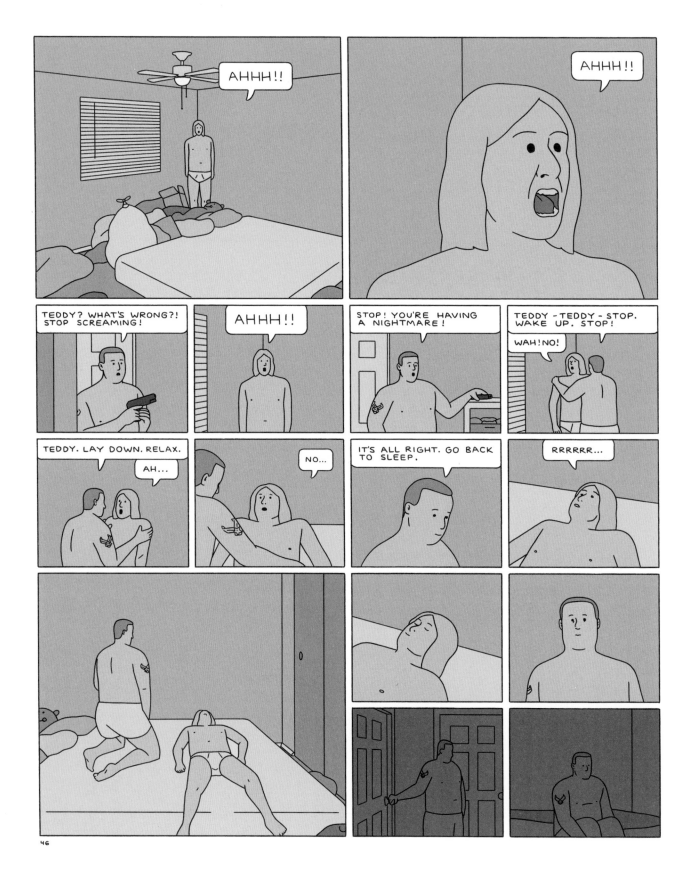

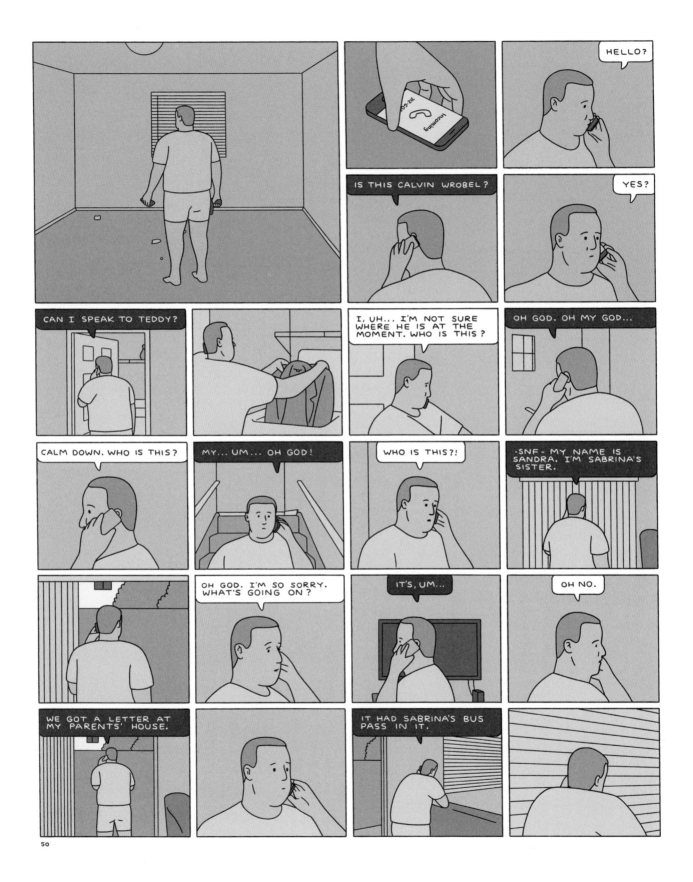

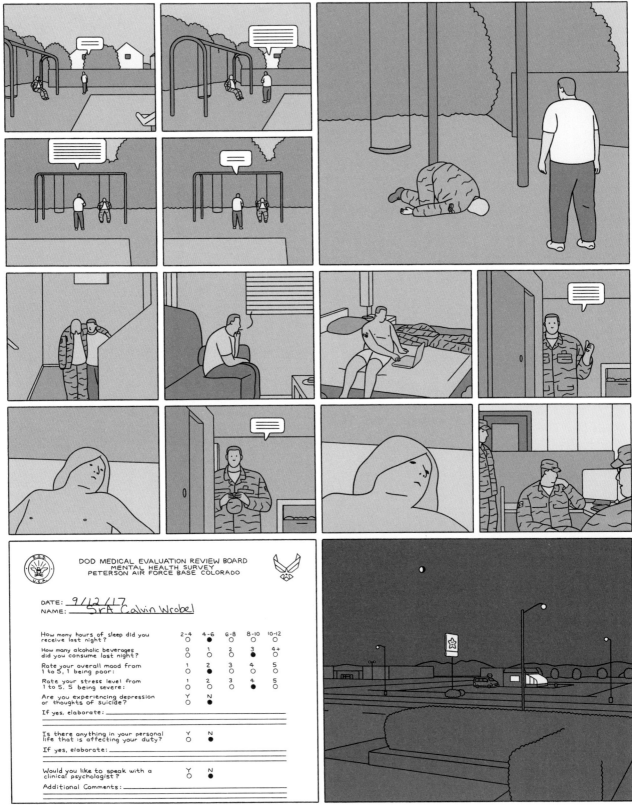

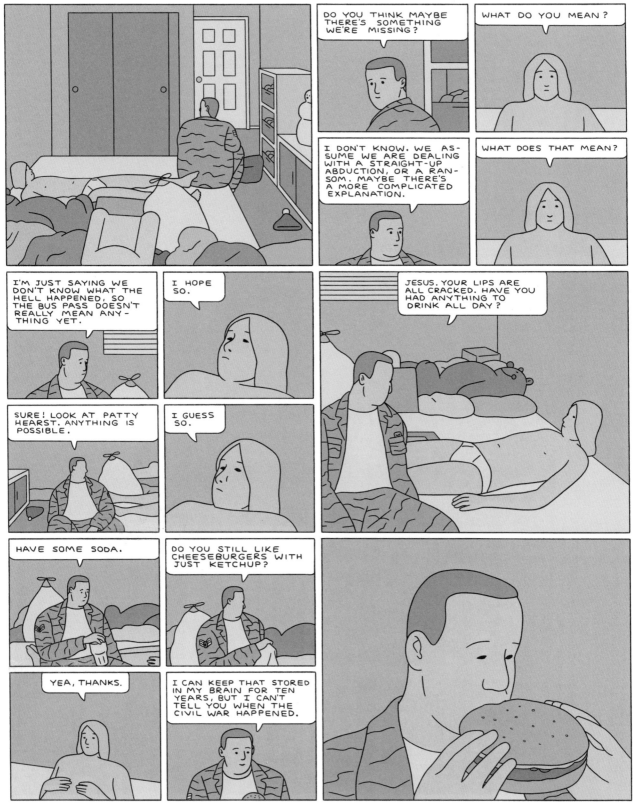

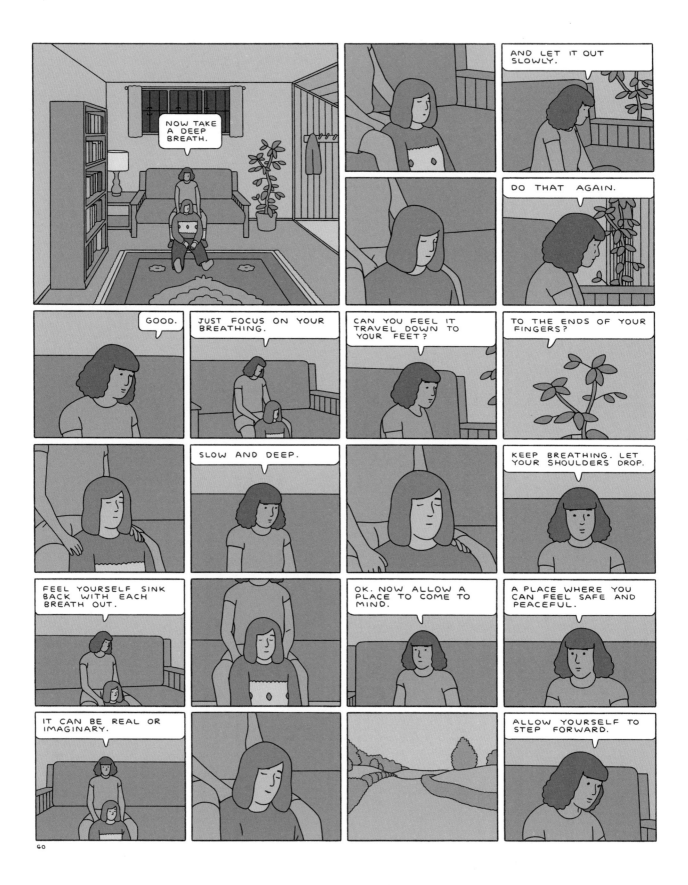

63

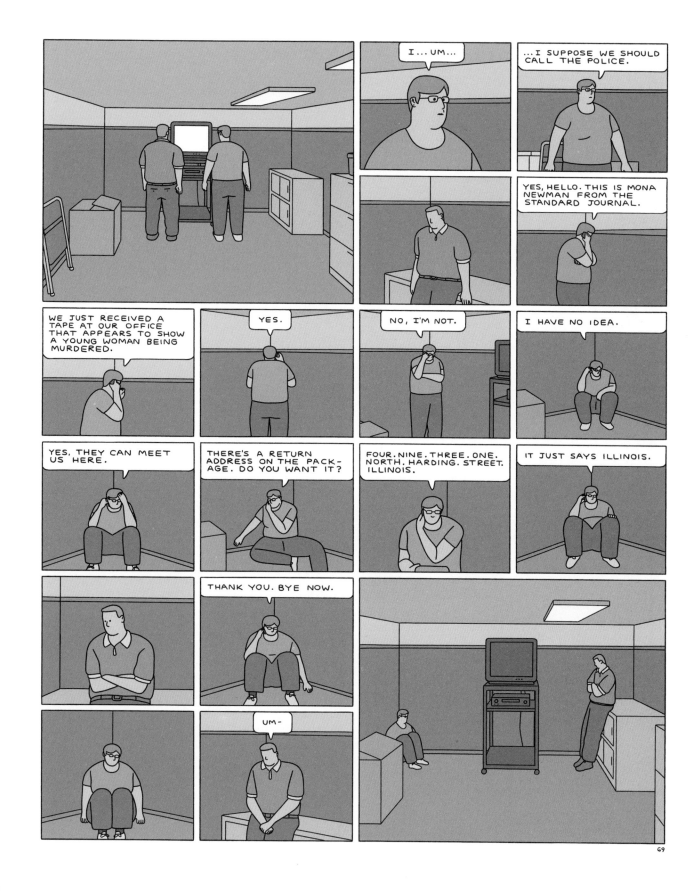

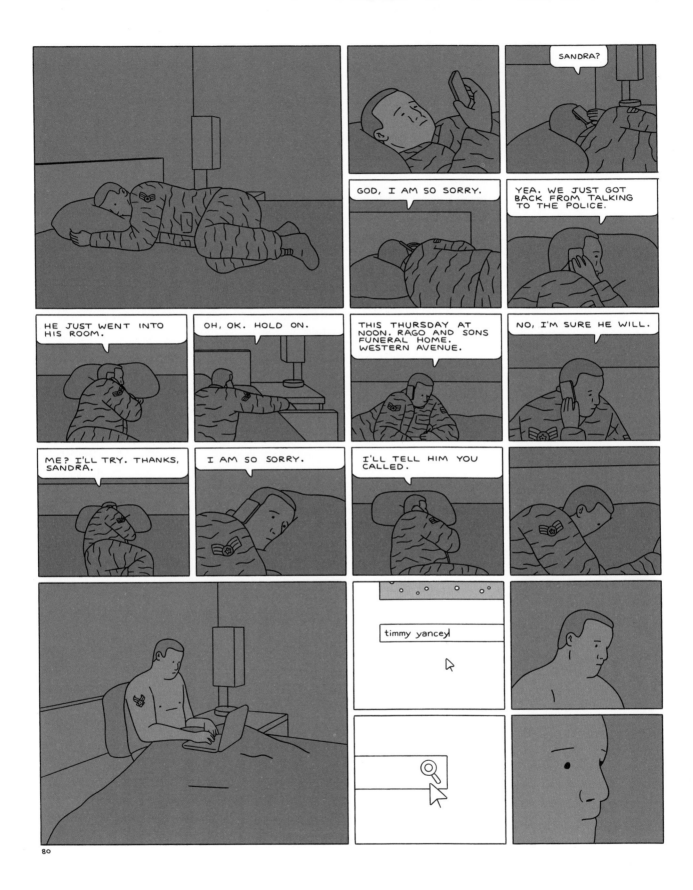

what happens next will shock you

You don't want to know what this economist predicts for 2018

Teen surprises mom and toddler with good deed at mall

A Northwest-Indiana teen is being praised on social media after his random act of kindness went viral.

It all began when Beth Russell, a resident of Portage, was birthday shopping with her youngest daughter, Paige.

As the two-year-old scanned the aisles of toys, her eyes fixed on a blonde doll, the last one on the shelf.

Before she could show her mom the doll, a young man walked over and asked if it was her favorite. She told the stranger that her birthday was approaching, and that she really loved the doll.

The teen laughed, grabbed the doll and left the aisle.

A few minutes later, the young man returned to the aisle with a bag under his arm. He handed Paige's mom a receipt, took the doll out of the bag and wished Paige a happy birthday.

Russell was at a loss for words. After a moment, she managed to thank him for the gift. The teen nodded, smiled and walked off. Before he was out of sight, Russell ushered him back to take a photo with Paige.

That night, Russell shared the story with her friends on Facebook, posting the photo of Paige with the young man, hoping that someone would be able to identify him.

After thousands of shares, someone recognized the teen as Centell Rodgers III, a senior football player at Horace Mann High School.

Russell thanked him again, for showing her daughter that hope is not lost on society as a whole.

Her hope is that sharing this story will inspire others to do good in the community.

"This extraordinary young man has taught Paige a meaningful life lesson. I'm so grateful for that."

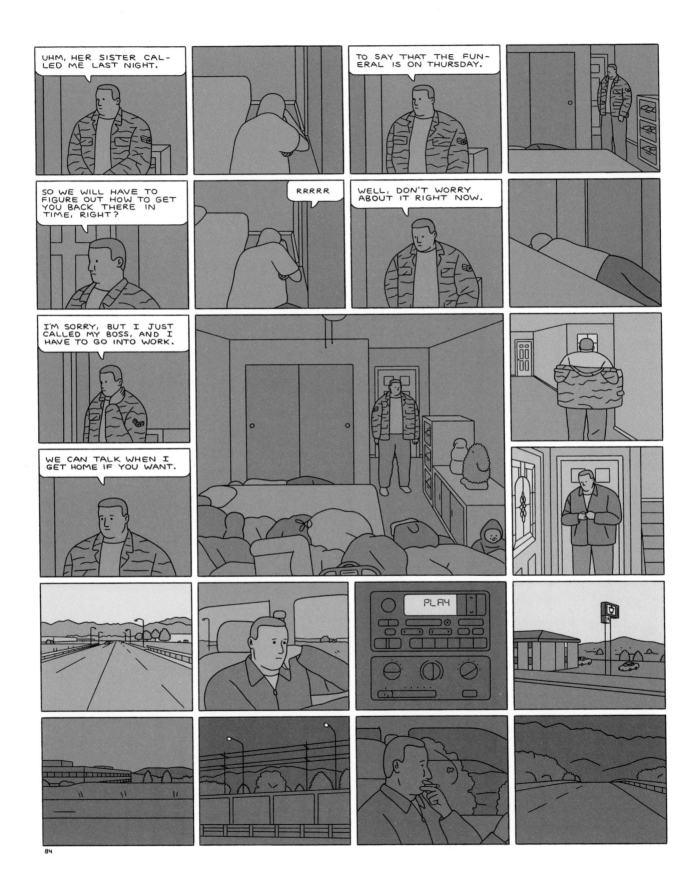

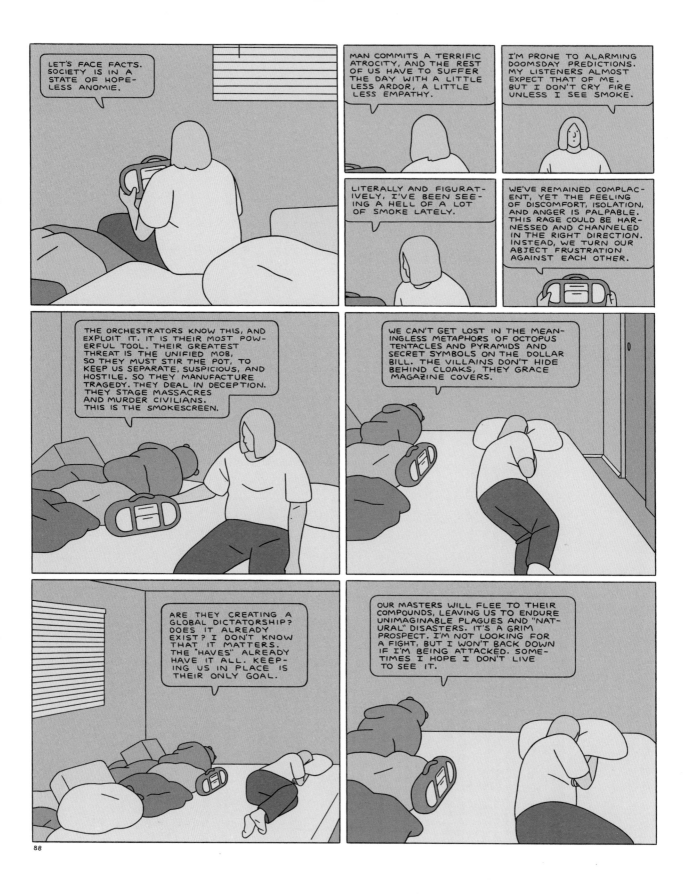

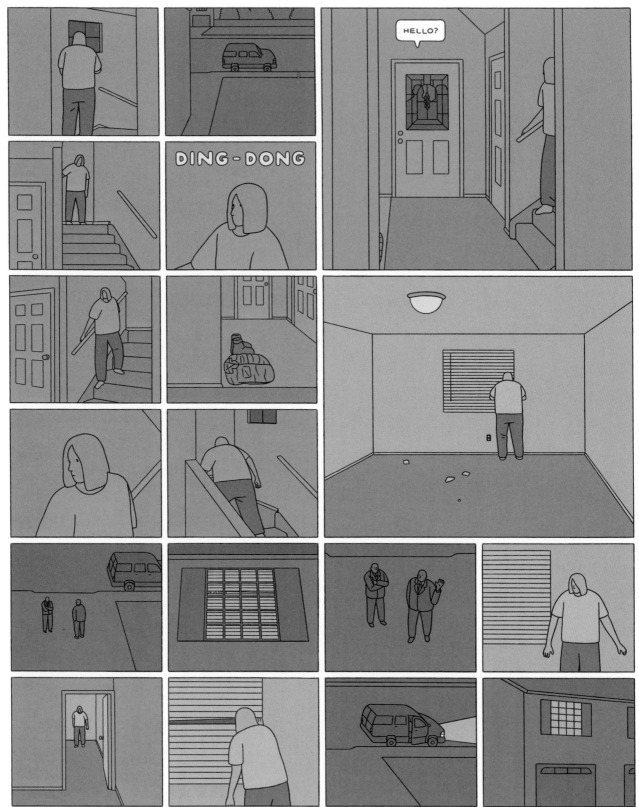

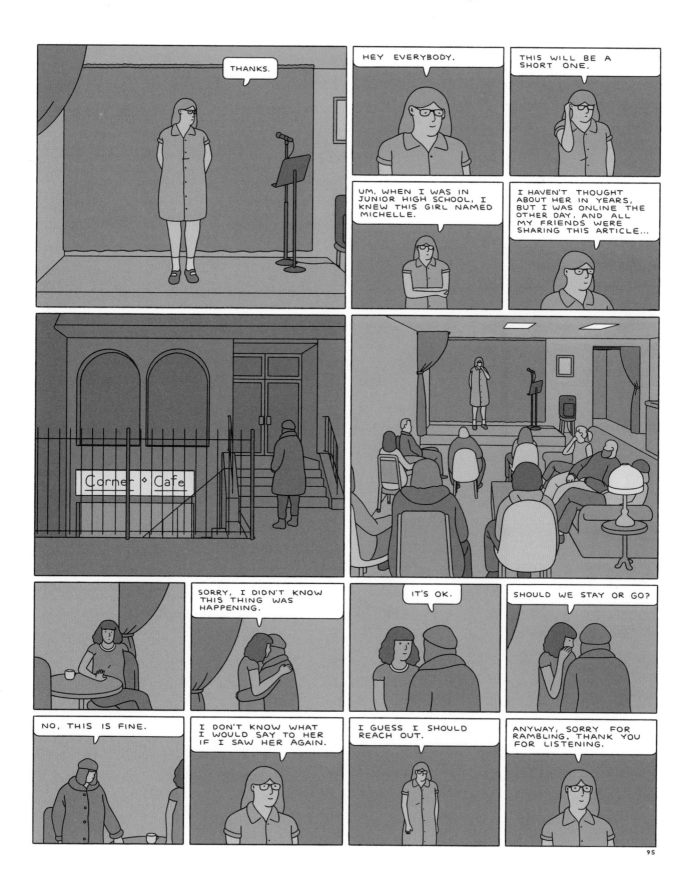

99

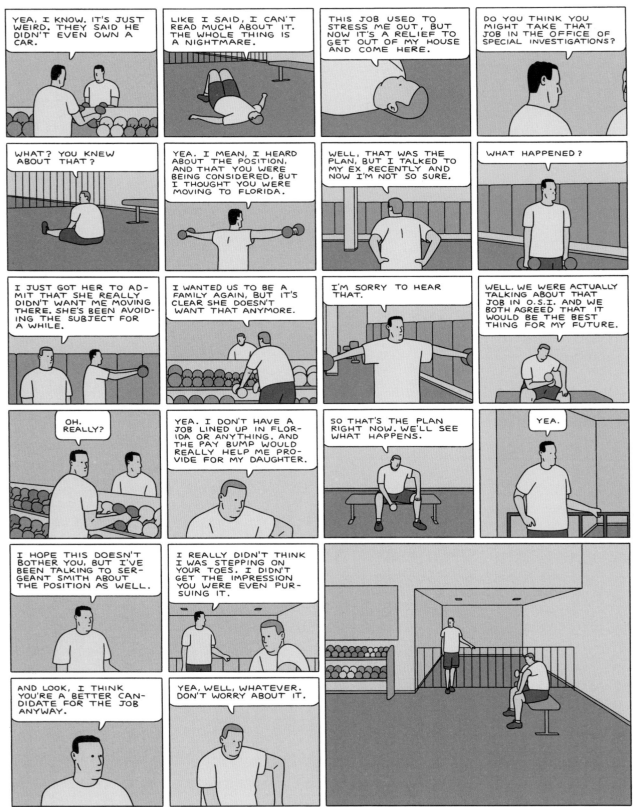

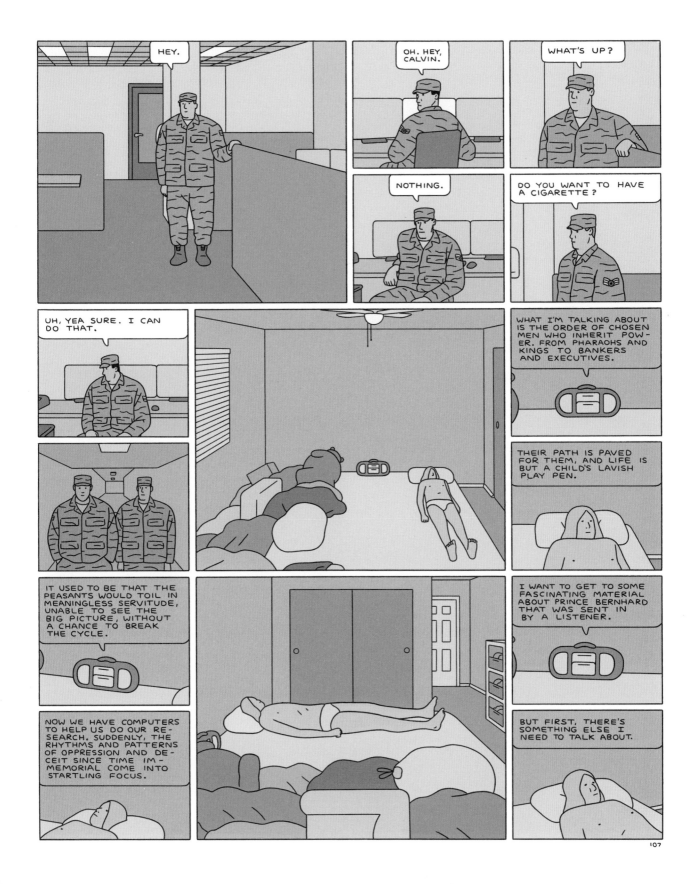

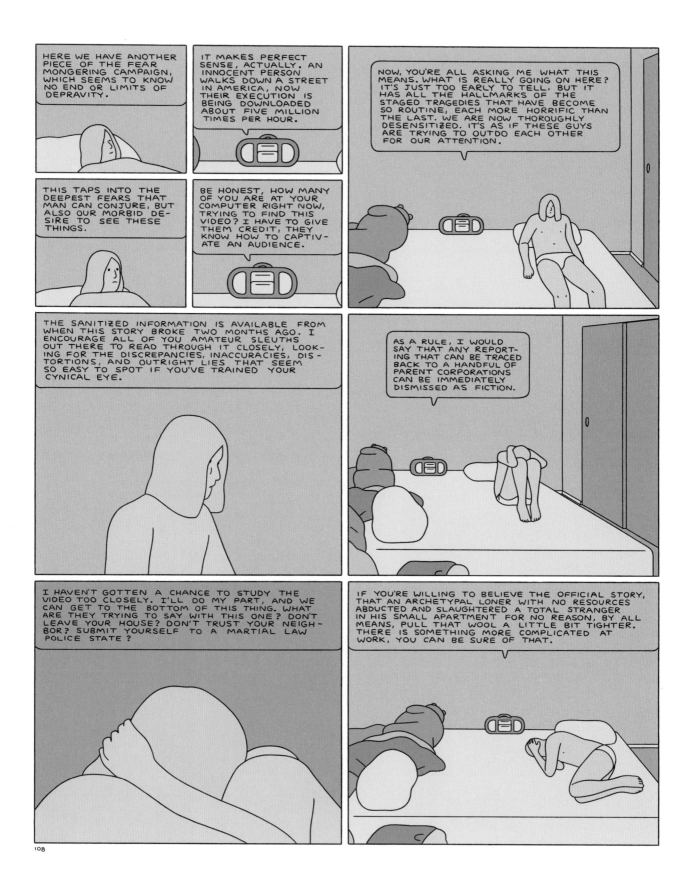

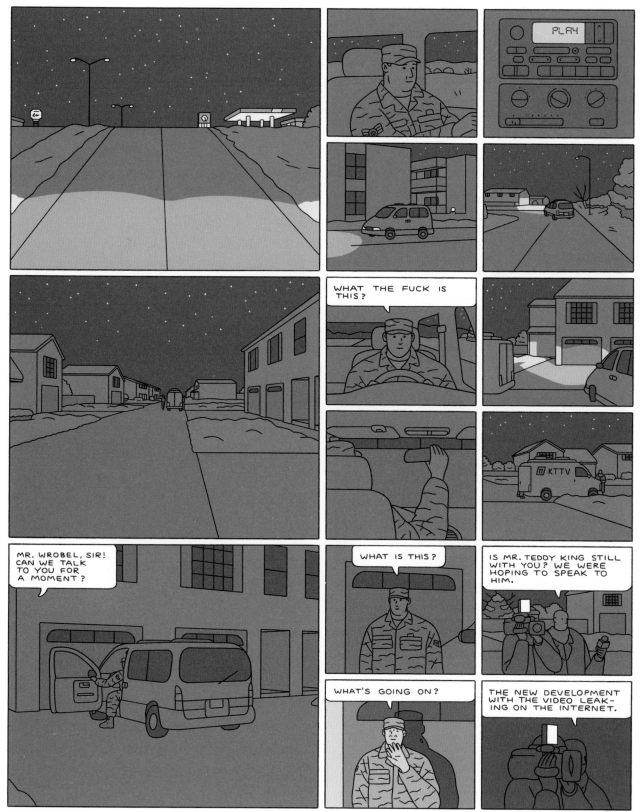

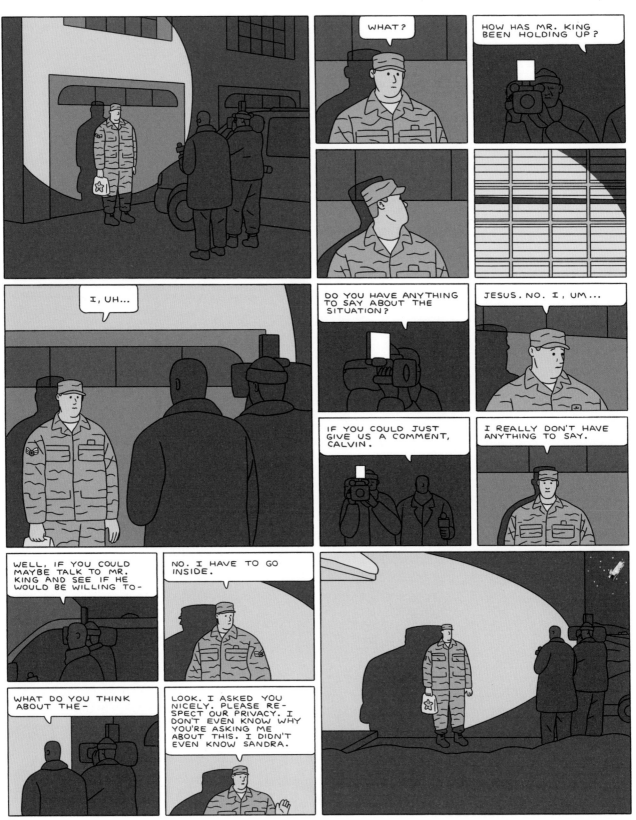

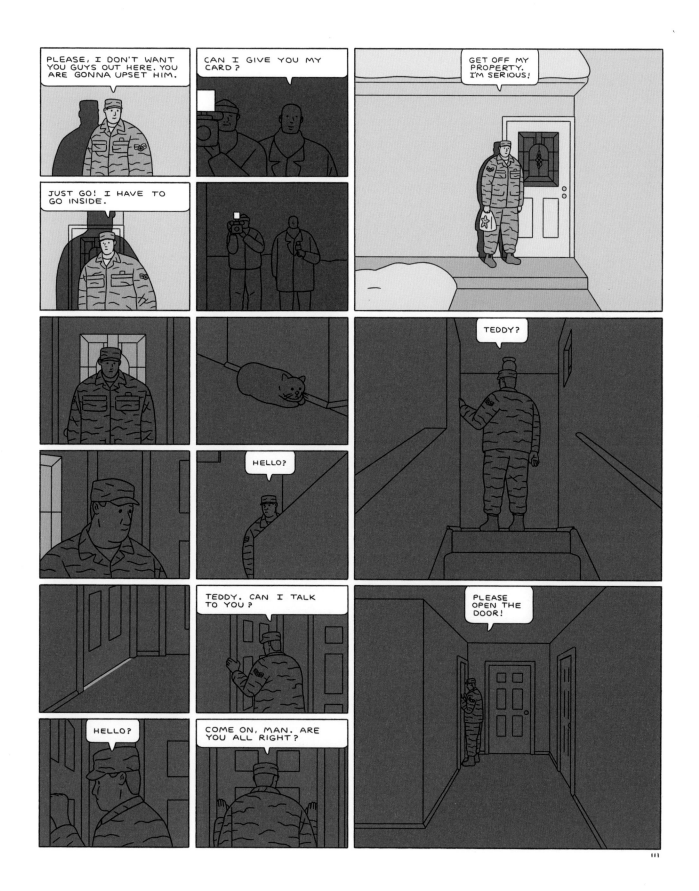

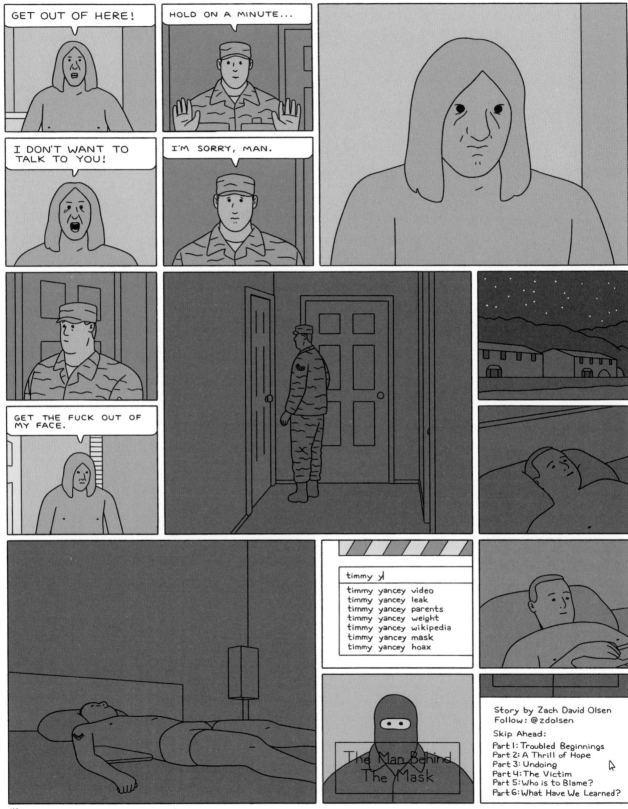

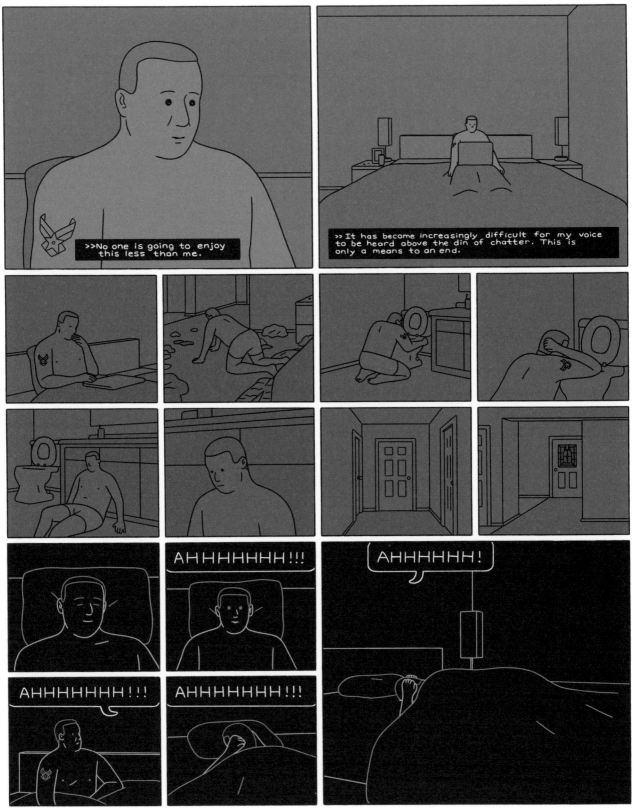

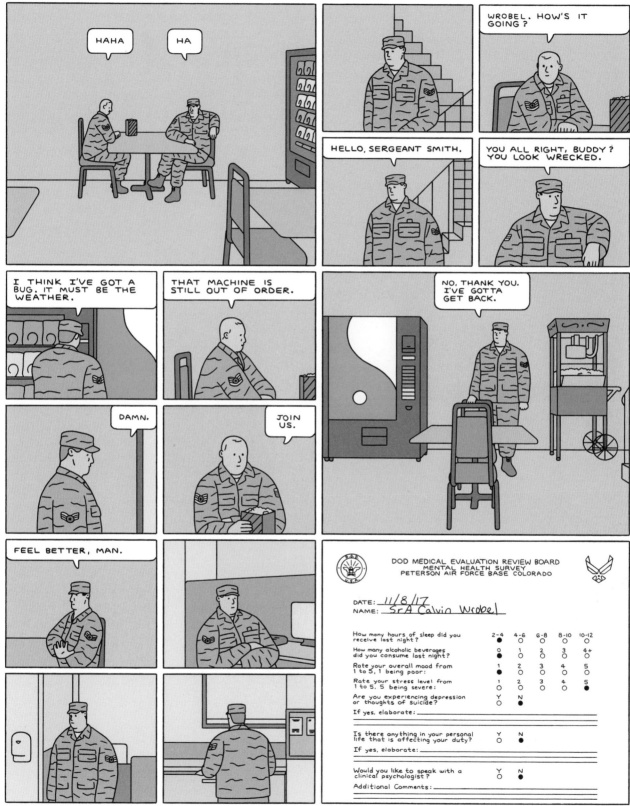

WELL, HERE WE ARE. WELCOME TO THE SHOW EVERYBODY.

WE'VE HAD SOME BEAUTIFUL WEATHER LATELY. CRISP AND REFRESHING. HOPE YOU'RE ALL ENJOYING IT AS MUCH AS I AM.

LET'S NOT WASTE ANY TIME. THE VIDEO FROM CHICAGO IS ON EVERYONE'S MIND.

THE MAINSTREAM MEDIA ARE CALLING IT THE MOST SADISTIC ACT OF RANDOM VIOLENCE WE'VE SEEN DOMESTICALLY IN DECADES. THE INTERNET IS RIFE WITH RUMORS AND SPECULATION. WE ARE ALL SEARCHING FOR MEANING.

LIKE MANY OF YOU, I RECOILED IN DISGUST. IT IS TRULY A TERRIFYING SIGHT. BUT YOU MUST RESIST YOUR INITIAL REACTION. DON'T LET THEM MANIPULATE YOUR EMOTIONS. TRY TO EXAMINE IT LIKE A FROG IN FORMALDEHYDE.

THERE ARE CERTAIN NAGGING QUESTIONS WE MUST CONSIDER. YANCEY'S WEIGHT WHEN HE DIED WAS REPORTEDLY ONE-HUNDRED-TEN POUNDS. DOES THE MAN IN THE VIDEO APPEAR TO WEIGH ONE-HUNDRED-TEN POUNDS?

WHY DOES HE STOP RECORDING AT ONE POINT, AND APPEAR TO TALK TO SOMEONE OFF-CAMERA? ARE THESE THE RAMBLINGS OF A DISTURBED YOUNG MAN, OR THE FINAL MOMENTS OF TWO PEOPLE HELD HOSTAGE?

I'M ALSO WONDERING WHY HE WOULD HIDE HIS FACE BEHIND A MASK IF HE CRAVED NOTORIETY FOR HIS CRIME. IS IT BECAUSE HE'S NOT THE EXECUTIONER AT ALL?

IT'S ALSO WORTH POINTING OUT THAT MANY LINES FROM HIS TIRADE WERE TAKEN FROM HIS OWN PAST WRITINGS ON DIFFERENT ONLINE FORUMS. WHY WOULD HE REUSE THINGS HE'D ALREADY SAID? LEADS ME TO BELIEVE HIS SPEECH WAS DRAFTED BY SOMEONE WHO WANTED TO MAKE IT APPEAR TO BE WRITTEN BY HIM.

I WON'T MINCE WORDS: I DON'T BELIEVE FOR A SECOND THAT SABRINA GALLO WAS KILLED BY TIMMY YANCEY. THE VIDEO JUST LOOKS UNBELIEVABLE. I DON'T BELIEVE SOMETHING LIKE THAT COULD HAPPEN.

FOR ALL WE KNOW, SHE'S ALIVE IN BONDAGE SOMEWHERE. OR SHE COULD BE AN ACTRESS WEARING PROSTHETICS TO CONCEAL HER IDENTITY. IT'S POSSIBLE SHE NEVER EVEN EXISTED. WE KNOW THE MILITARY HAS ACCESS TO ADVANCED COMPUTER-GENERATED IMAGE TECHNOLOGY THAT THE PUBLIC WON'T BE AWARE OF FOR ANOTHER TEN YEARS.

MAYBE FORCES TOO EVIL TO COMPREHEND DID IN FACT MURDER A WOMAN NAMED SABRINA GALLO. I JUST DON'T THINK A MAN NAMED TIMMY YANCEY IS RESPONSIBLE.

WHEN THE HYSTERIA SUBSIDES, THIS VIDEO IS DESTINED TO BE ANOTHER RELIC THAT WE WILL NEVER TRULY UNDERSTAND. A NEW TRAGEDY PRESENTS ITSELF BEFORE WE CAN MAKE SENSE OF THE LAST. WHY DOES THIS KEEP HAPPENING, AND WHO KEEPS DOING THIS TO US? I WISH I COULD STRANGLE THEIR COLLECTIVE NECKS AND BE DONE WITH IT, SO WE COULD BUILD OUR UTOPIA IN PEACE. MAYBE SOME ADVANCED BEING WILL SIFT THROUGH THIS JUNK WHEN WE'RE GONE, AND WONDER HOW SIBLINGS COULD BE SO CRUEL TO EACH OTHER.

NOTHING JUST HAPPENS. EVERY NEWS STORY IS AS STRATEGICALLY MANUFACTURED AS THE ADS WEDGED BETWEEN THEM. THERE'S A STORY ABOUT HOUSING PRICES. THERE'S A COMMERCIAL OFFERING CASH FOR GOLD. THERE'S A STORY ABOUT A MASS SHOOTING. THERE'S A COMMERCIAL FOR ANTIDEPRESSANTS. WHEN YOU'RE WILLING TO ACKNOWLEDGE THESE PATTERNS, YOU MIGHT NEVER SLEEP SOUNDLY AGAIN.

THE FEAR OF THE UNKNOWN, THAT DEATH COULD STRIKE IN THE SAFEST PLACE, IS ESSENTIAL TO THE PARANOIA CAMPAIGN. THINK ABOUT IT. IN THE PAST FEW YEARS WE'VE SEEN ATTACKS IN A GRADE SCHOOL, A MOVIE THEATER, A CHURCH, A HOSPITAL, AND NEARLY EVERYWHERE IN BETWEEN. DOESN'T THIS TIMMY YANCEY THING SEEM LIKE PART OF AN ESCALATING CONTINUUM?

GIVEN THE GROSS ATROCITIES OF THE SHADOW GOVERNMENT THAT ARE REVEALED AFTER THE FACT — SECRET WARS, ILLEGAL SURVEILLANCE, MIND CONTROL EXPERIMENTS AND THE LIKE — WOULD YOU PUT IT PAST THEM TO KILL ONE OR TWO INNOCENT CIVILIANS IF IT FURTHERED THEIR PLANS?

WHO ARE THESE AGENCIES BUT A COLLECTION OF EMPLOYEES, UNDER CONTRACT, CONCERNED ONLY WITH THEIR CAREERS AND REPUTATIONS? IF A MORAL OBJECTION MEANT LOSING YOUR JOB, YOUR HOME, EVEN YOUR LIFE — COULD YOU BLAME ANY OF THEM FOR THEIR OBEDIENCE? WOULD YOU ACT ANY DIFFERENT?

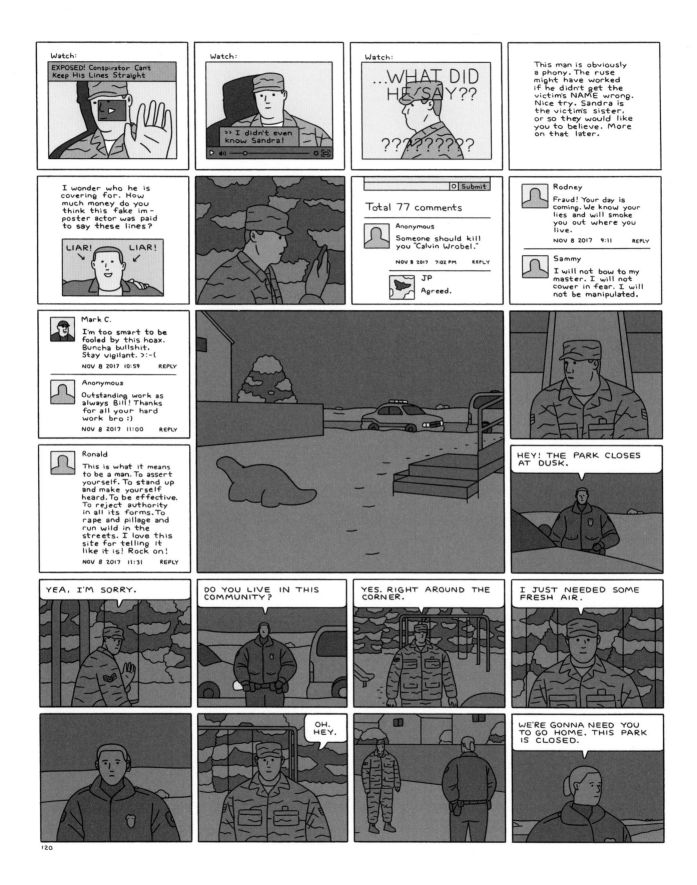

After Chicago Execution, 'False Flag' Conspiracy Theories Surface

By Molly O'Connell
November 8 2017

It is now expected that with any highly publicized act of violence comes dissidence and a host of alternative explanations.

A small but vocal minority believe that a global cabal is behind every major tragedy, from the death of a celebrity to the attacks of 9/11 to the murder of an innocent woman.

In the wake of the shooting at Sandy Hook Elementary in which twenty children and six adults were murdered by a single gunman, some parents of the victims were harassed by people who believed they were actors, that their children never even existed, and that they were paid to participate in the cover-up.

This may seem like marginal extremism, but to this day when you type "Sandy Hook" into Google, the first suggested word to add to the search phrase is "fake." The hysteria is spreading, and the reason for this varies wildly, depending on which side you ask.

The killing of Sabrina Gallo is no exception. Within hours, conspiracy websites were already labeling the execution video a hoax, claiming that it was "obviously designed as a fear-mongering distraction."

When a Louisville news program erroneously reported that a third body was found in Timmy Yancey's apartment, then quickly apologized for the mistake, conspiracy theorists used this as proof of deception.

When Calvin Wrobel, a friend of Sabrina Gallo's boyfriend, was stopped by a news crew outside his home last night and referred to the victim by the wrong name, that was used as proof positive of a conspiracy.

The problem with these theories is that they can't be reasoned with. Any fact that doesn't fit the alternative explanation is dismissed as a lie or disinformation. Any avoidance is tacit confirmation. Anyone close to the victim is an actor or being paid to remain silent.

The most troubling detail of the Timmy Yancey story is that he seemed to be a proponent of such radical conspiracy theories. We now know that he listened to the Albert Douglas radio show every day, and frequently wrote on the show's message board, showing support for the ideas espoused by the host.

Timmy Yancey was actually being mourned on one website as an innocent scapegoat that was targeted because of his political beliefs and his online presence in conspiracy theory circles. Concurrently, the same website demonized Sabrina Gallo and her family as somehow being insiders in the plot.

This morning, Sandra Gallo filed a police report, claiming that she received death threats from a man who demanded to know what really happened to her sister. Similar threats are being hurled at Sabrina Gallo's boyfriend, who has not made any public statements.

Despite being staunchly anti-government, Yancey had a curious preoccupation with the military. As a child, he immersed himself in World War II history, and often said he wished he could have been alive to fight. He even wanted to enlist in the army, but his mother discouraged him.

Radio host Albert Douglas served in the army during the Gulf War. It wasn't until after 9/11 and the invasion of Iraq that he became interested in conspiracy theories, and began broadcasting when he was laid off from his job as a postman in 2009.

Since then, he has built a sizable audience by routinely predicting an imminent apocalypse, and claiming that most acts of terrorism are staged by the government as a means to strip the American people of their freedom and push through stricter gun control legislation.

These theories have been given credence by writers and academics such as Harry Drake, a professor at Florida State University who was fired after asking the parents of a child murdered at Sandy Hook to produce a death certificate.

WOULD YOU LIKE ANYTHING ELSE?

NO, THANK YOU.

WE'RE CLOSING IN TWENTY MINUTES. YOU HAVE A GREAT NIGHT.

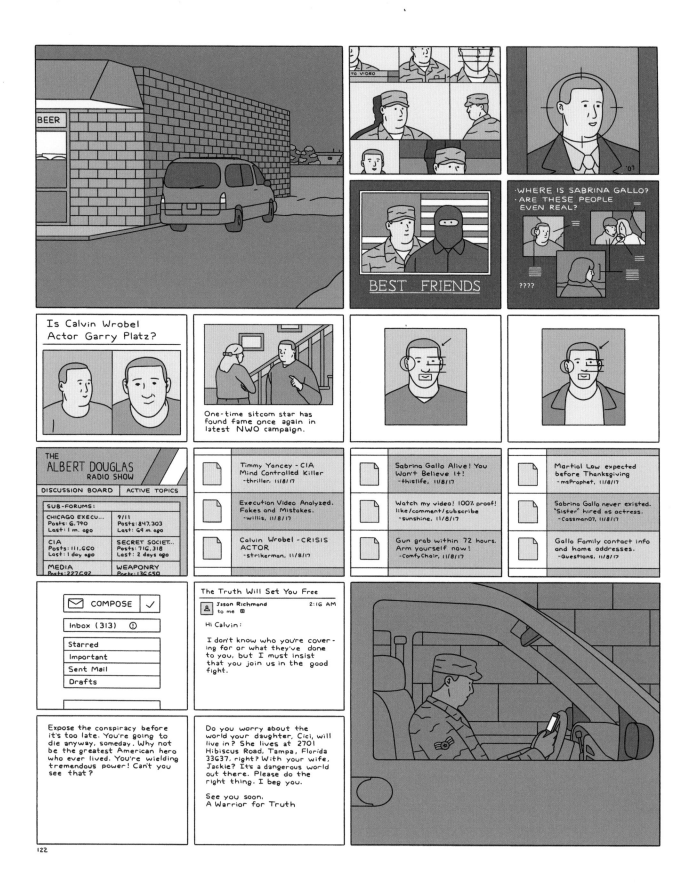

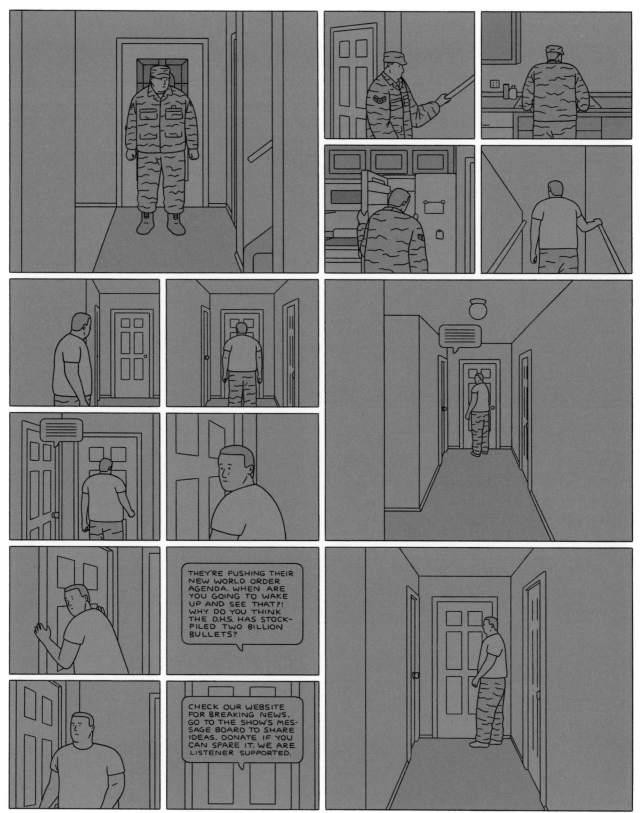

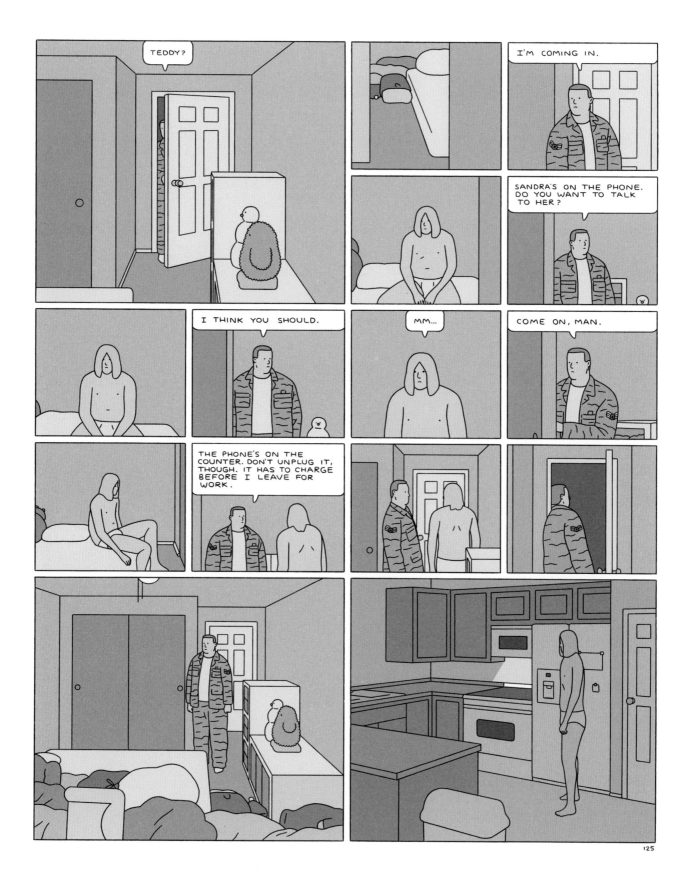

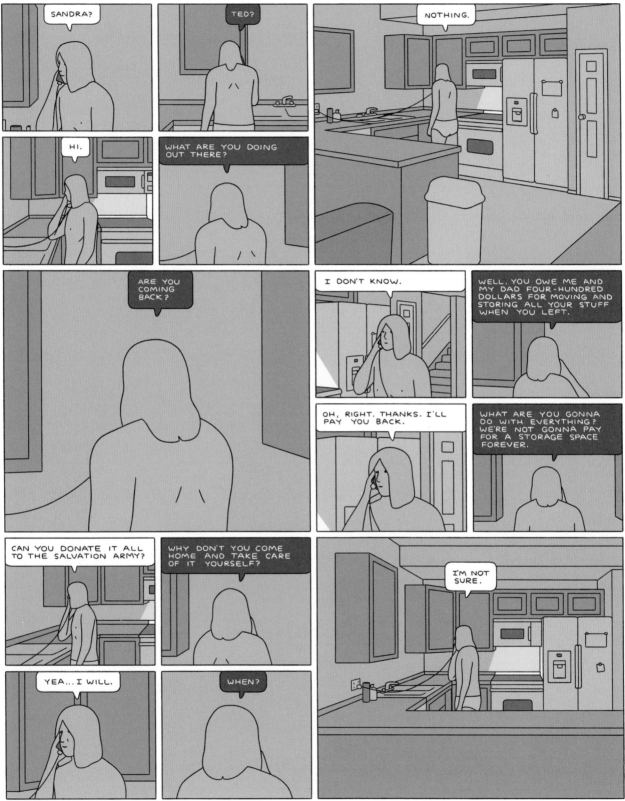

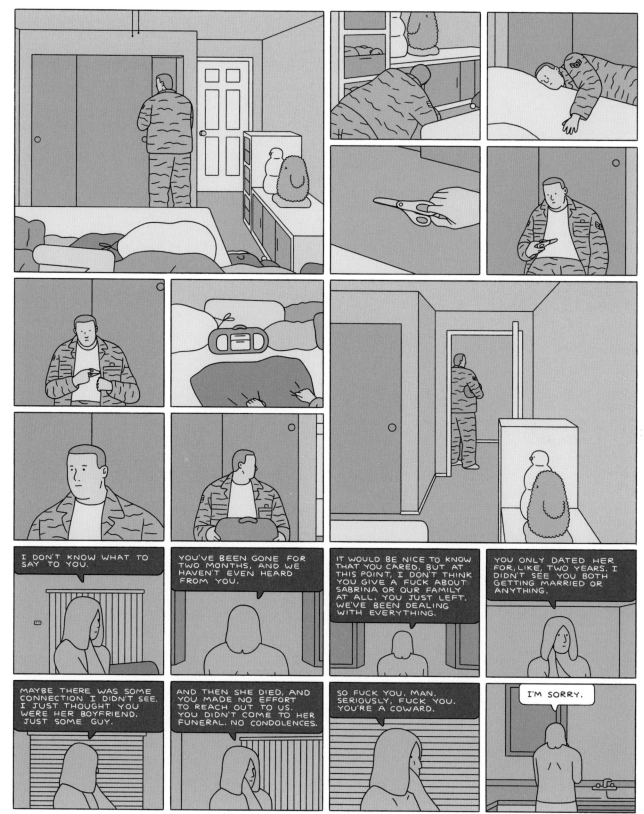

I DON'T KNOW WHAT TO SAY TO YOU.

YOU'VE BEEN GONE FOR TWO MONTHS, AND WE HAVEN'T EVEN HEARD FROM YOU.

IT WOULD BE NICE TO KNOW THAT YOU CARED, BUT AT THIS POINT, I DON'T THINK YOU GIVE A FUCK ABOUT SABRINA OR OUR FAMILY AT ALL. YOU JUST LEFT. WE'VE BEEN DEALING WITH EVERYTHING.

YOU ONLY DATED HER FOR, LIKE, TWO YEARS. I DIDN'T SEE YOU BOTH GETTING MARRIED OR ANYTHING.

MAYBE THERE WAS SOME CONNECTION I DIDN'T SEE. I JUST THOUGHT YOU WERE HER BOYFRIEND. JUST SOME GUY.

AND THEN SHE DIED, AND YOU MADE NO EFFORT TO REACH OUT TO US. YOU DIDN'T COME TO HER FUNERAL. NO CONDOLENCES.

SO FUCK YOU, MAN. SERIOUSLY, FUCK YOU. YOU'RE A COWARD.

I'M SORRY.

☑ COMPOSE ✓

Inbox (631)

Starred

Important

Sent Mail

Drafts

Good News

👤 Jason Richmond   4:50 PM
to me ▣

Hey Calvin!

Read this article I found. Fascinating stuff! I hope you've been thinking about what I wrote to you last night.

Your friend,
Truth Warrior

One-thousand miles south of Hawaii lies the US-controlled Palmyra Atoll.

Once used as a naval station during World War II, it has mostly been privately owned, until the year 2000, when the Nature Conservancy purchased Palmyra for thirty-million dollars.

Since then, small research teams have inhabited Palmyra on a rotating basis. There are no permanent residents or significant infrastructure. All the roads that were created by the Navy have overgrown and become unusable. That's the simple story of this forgotten tropical paradise.

This is not the truth.

The atoll is actually a "black site," used by the US government as a secret prison. I know this because I've been there.

I was on a flight from Los Angeles to Sydney, Australia, falling in and out of sleep, drowsy from my medication. I awoke to an announcement. We had to make an emergency landing at an airstrip south of Hawaii. Through later research, I surmised that this could have only been Palmyra Atoll.

I felt sick and asked to be taken off the plane. The air smelled good and the water was clear. Little animals scurried about. To my surprise, we came upon a community of clean, well-dressed English speakers. They appeared to be well cared for and in good spirits.

I asked what they were doing there and this is what I was told.

They were all abducted under similar circumstances. Few seemed to understand why they were targeted, but the general feeling was that the US government and the CIA were somehow behind their captivity.

I was told that, among the inhabitants, there was an entire classroom of children and a subway train of strangers that found themselves kidnapped, hooded, and dropped on the atoll. Their captors gave no explanation, and they've never received news from the outside world.

Upon arrival, they are vaccinated and tested for diseases. They are sterilized to control the population. They are told that those who choose to cooperate will live out their days in isolated bliss, wanting for nothing, working for no one. Those who refuse are summarily executed.

New captives are shaken and frightened, but welcomed warmly by the small community. They are never abused in the adjustment process, simply allowed to adapt peacefully to their new reality.

They are not under lock and key. There is no supervision. There are no guards. So far as I could tell, there are no laws put in place by the captors. It seems that the community succeeds or fails by its own moral code.

They don't behave like prisoners. There is no hierarchy. No one is in charge or superior to anyone else. They didn't even ask to leave or help them escape or send word to their families. One man said he had been there for forty years.

I was told that many happy couples have found love on the compound. They live in comfortable, small wooden homes. There are generators for refrigeration and light. Food is delivered regularly, and a doctor visits once a month.

Books are sometimes dropped off as well, and a small library has been amassed. Most of them seem to have come from public libraries in the American Midwest, where I'm from. There was a book from my hometown library. I checked the circulation card and found the name of my third grade teacher.

I asked a teenage girl if there was a message she wanted to send back to civilization. She said "no."

We were back in the air within an hour, this strange encounter a foggy memory as I drifted back to sleep.

I've tried to revisit the colony, but charter flights are not allowed to land on the air strip. Officially, the atoll is used exclusively as a conservation research center, but I know the truth.

Now, when I see an atrocity unfold on the news, I wonder if the victims are bound and gagged on a flight to Palmyra. It would not surprise me if the dead at Sandy Hook, the Boston Marathon, and Sabrina Gallo were now living together, totally unaware of the impact they are having on the world.

It leaves me to wonder. Maybe, as I write this, Sabrina Gallo sits in the sand, watching the sunset. Maybe she'll walk back to the common area where people gather for dinner and play cards under generated light. Maybe she will outlive all of us. It helps me sleep to consider these pleasant scenarios.

I hope you believe that I mean what I say.

I am writing a book about my experience on Palmyra Atoll that will be self-published in the spring of 2018. Donations and pre-orders are welcomed and greatly appreciated. ▢

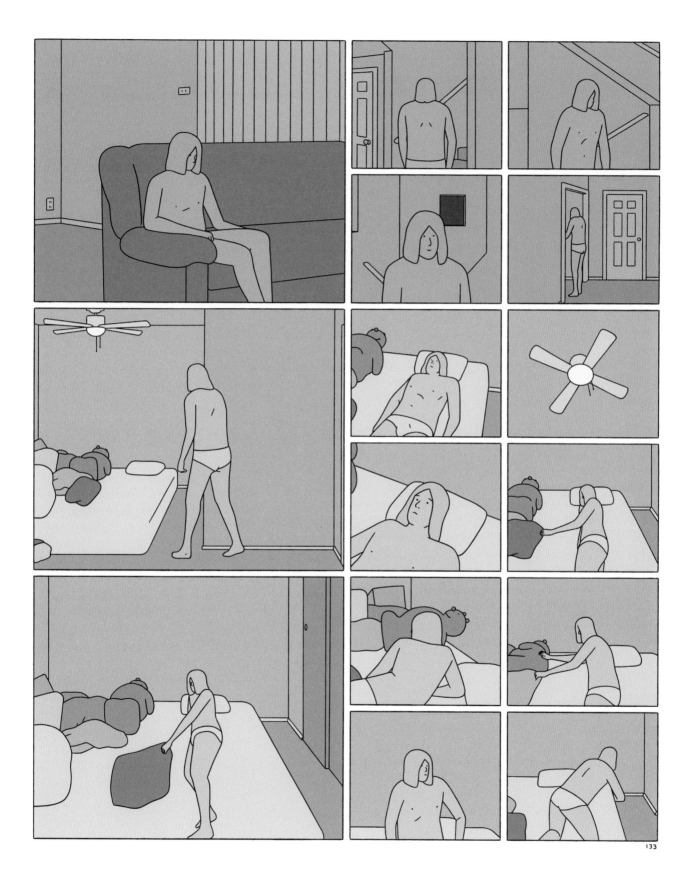

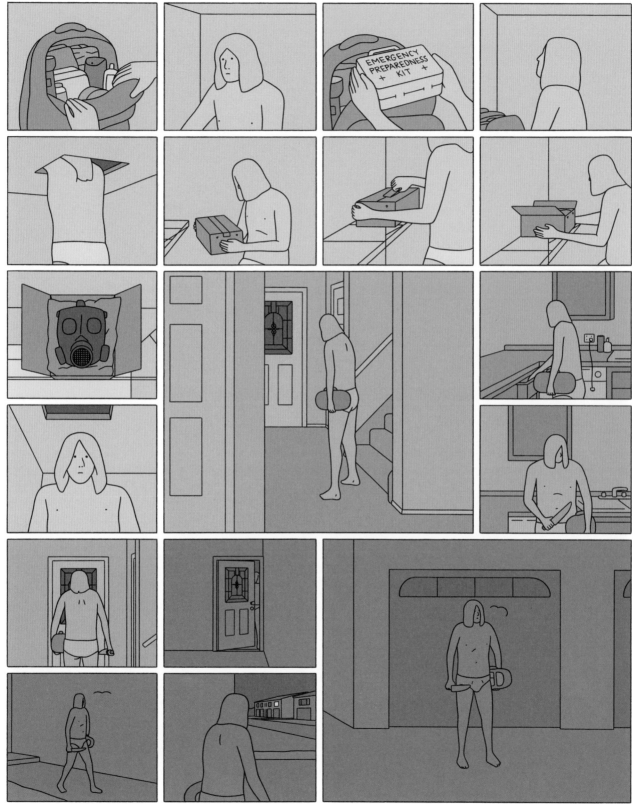

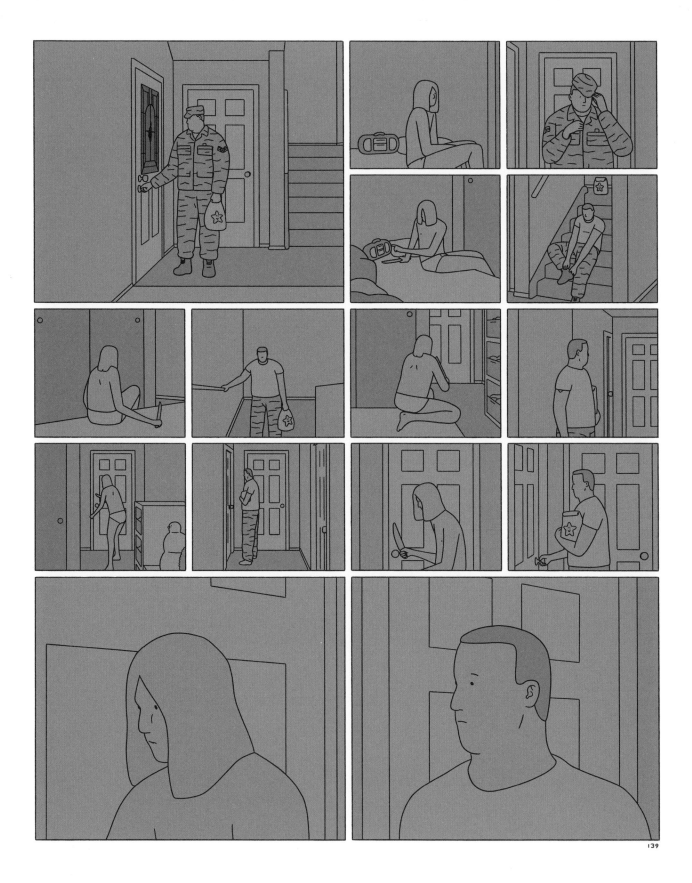

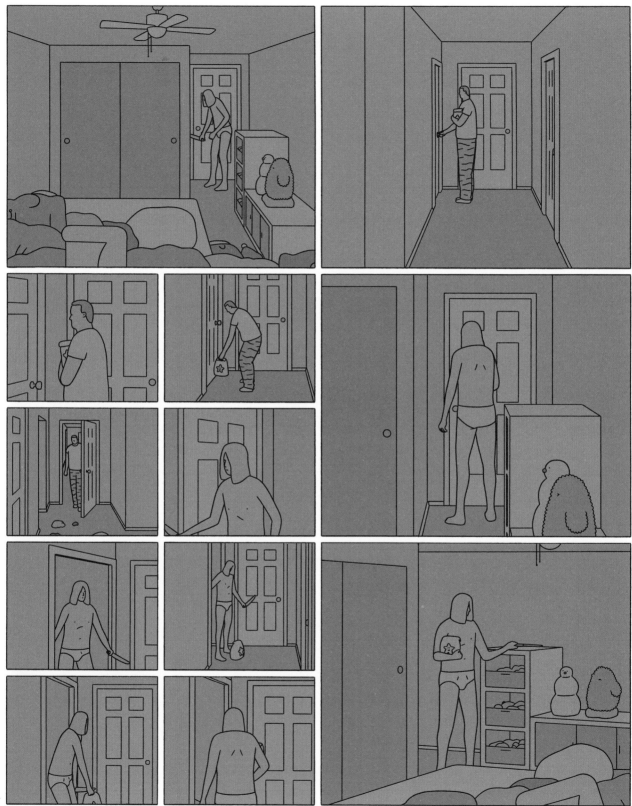

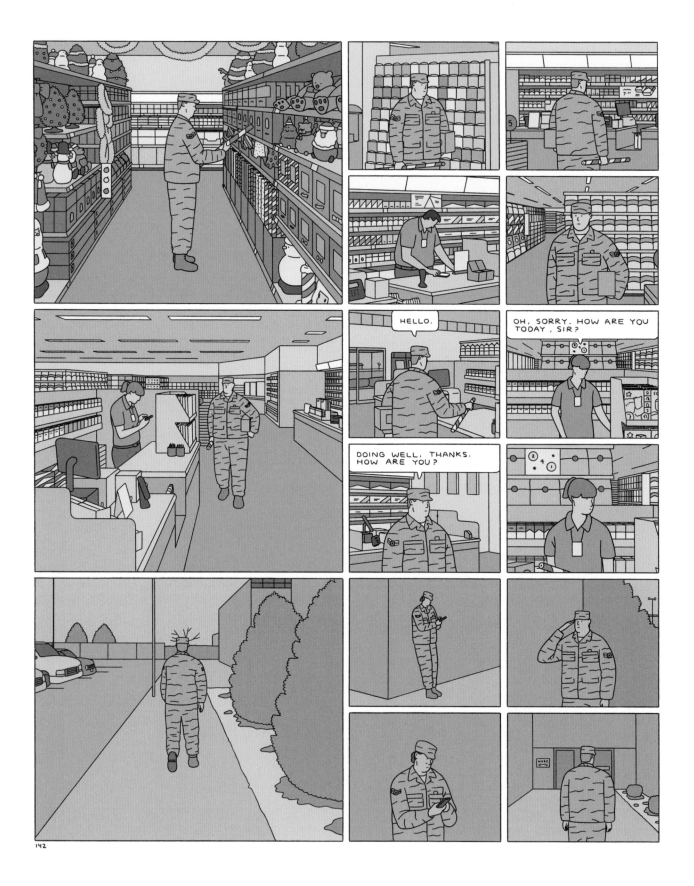

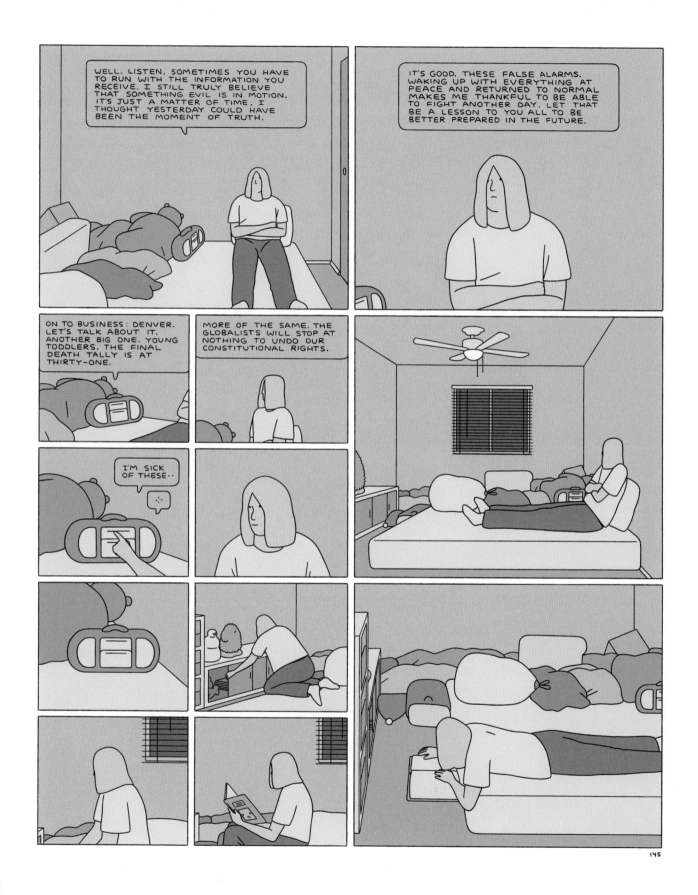

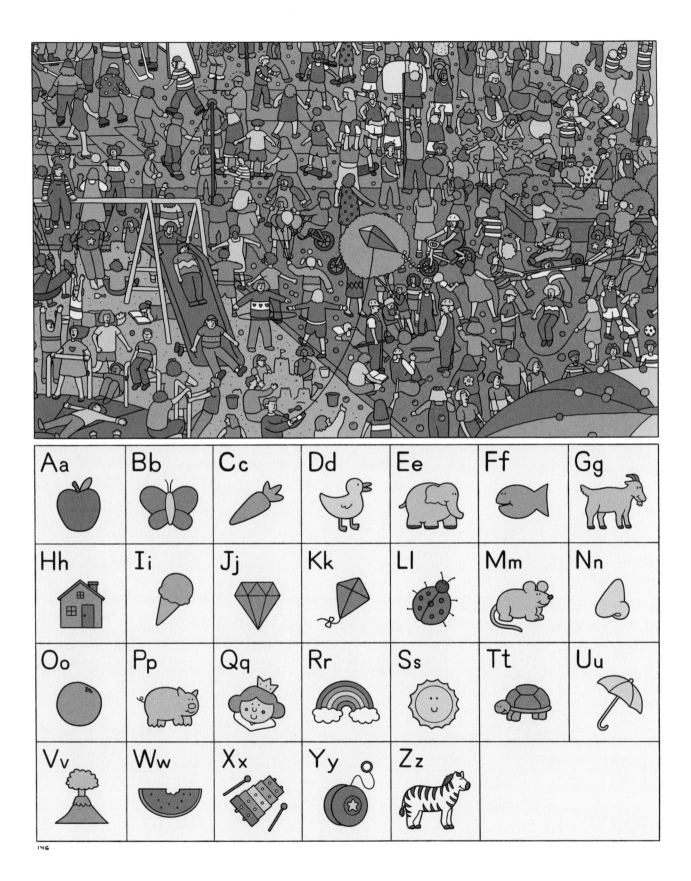

150

159

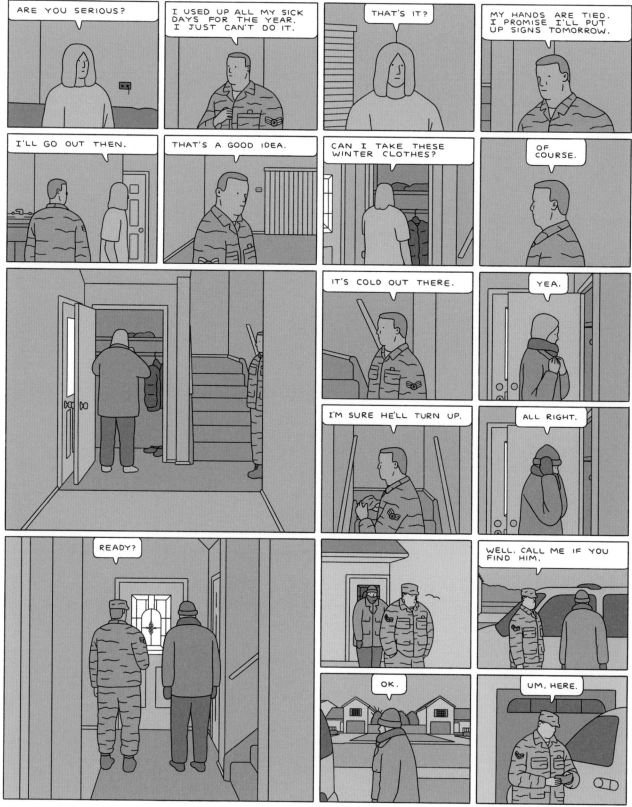

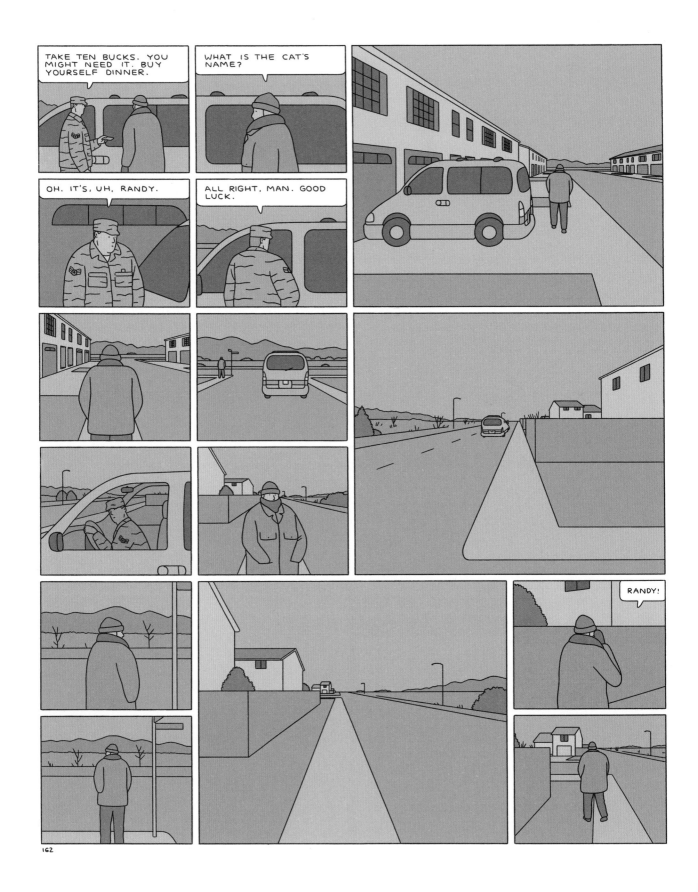

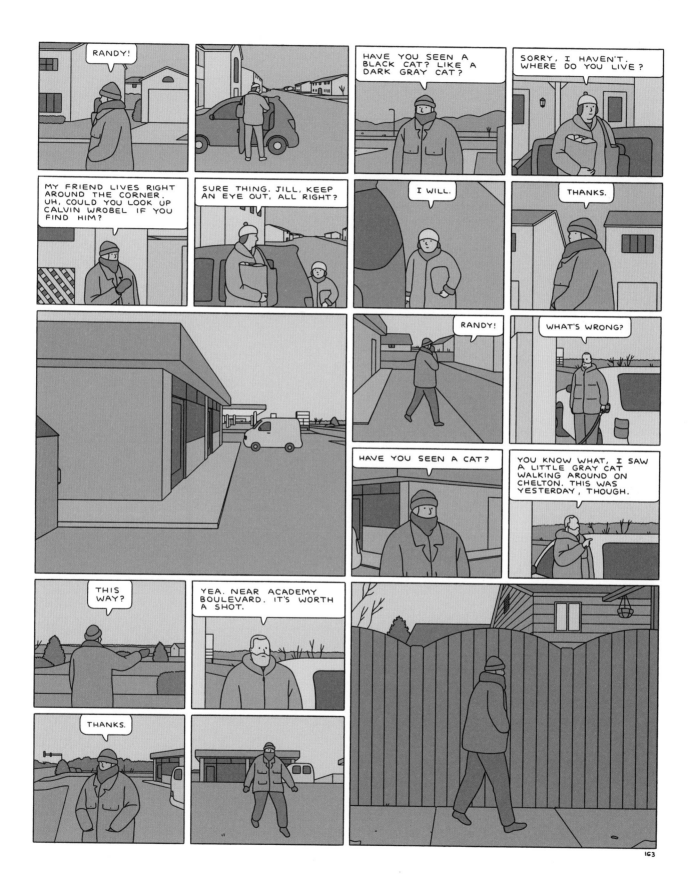

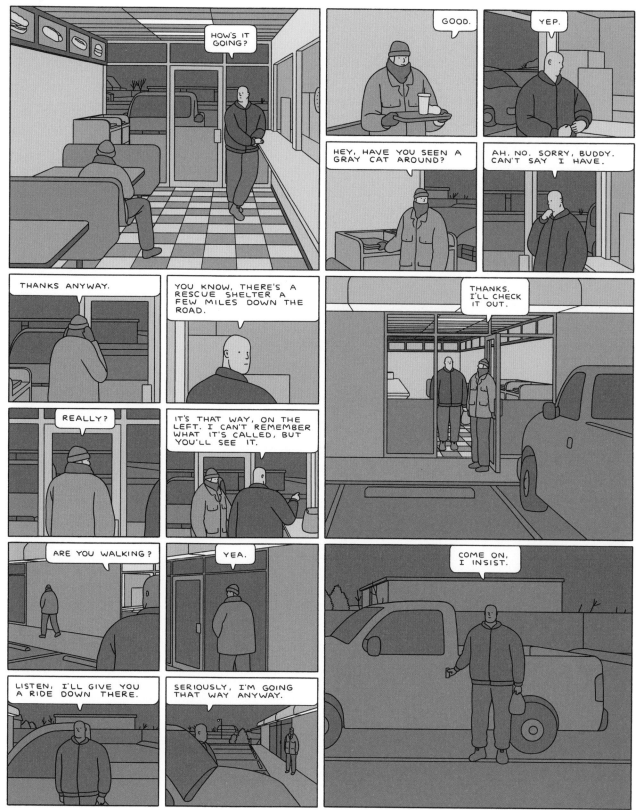

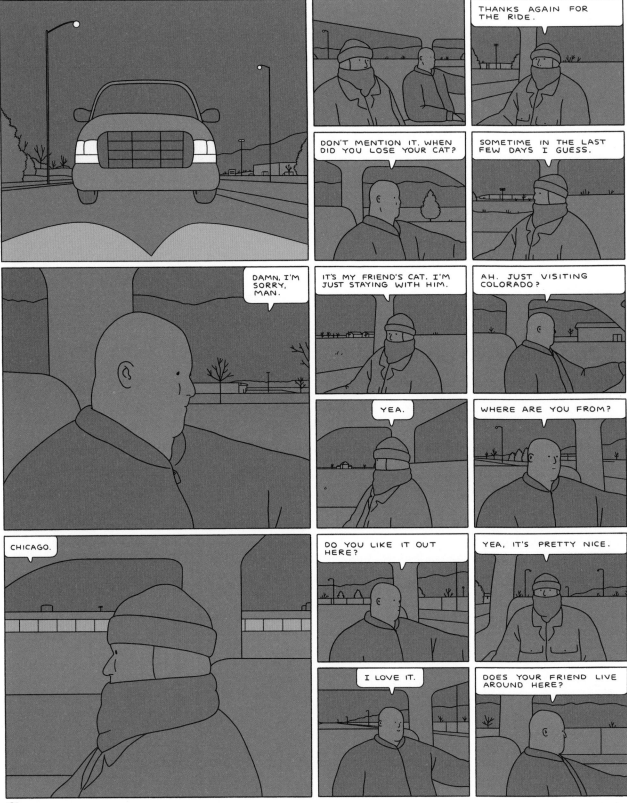

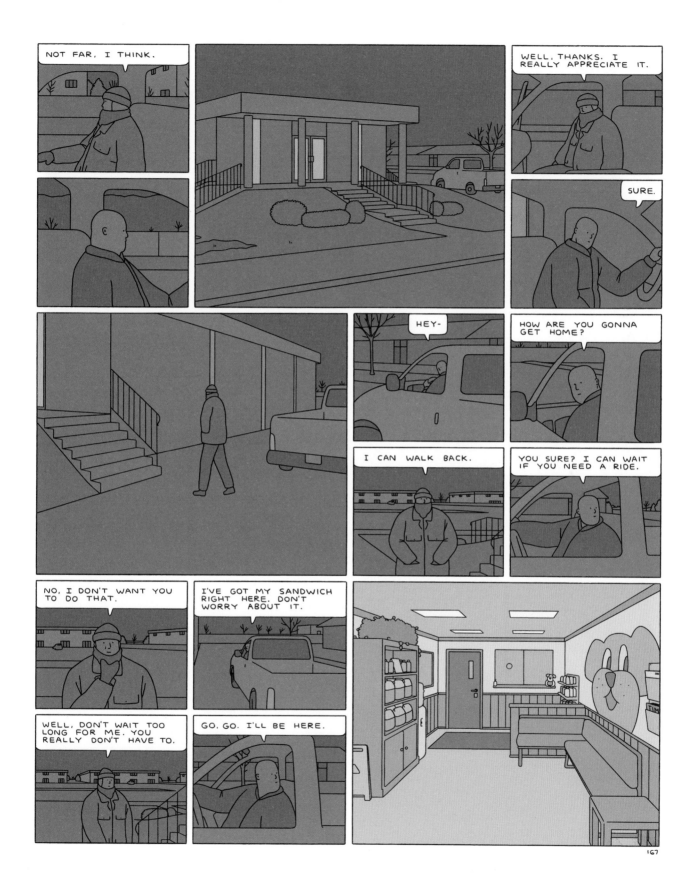

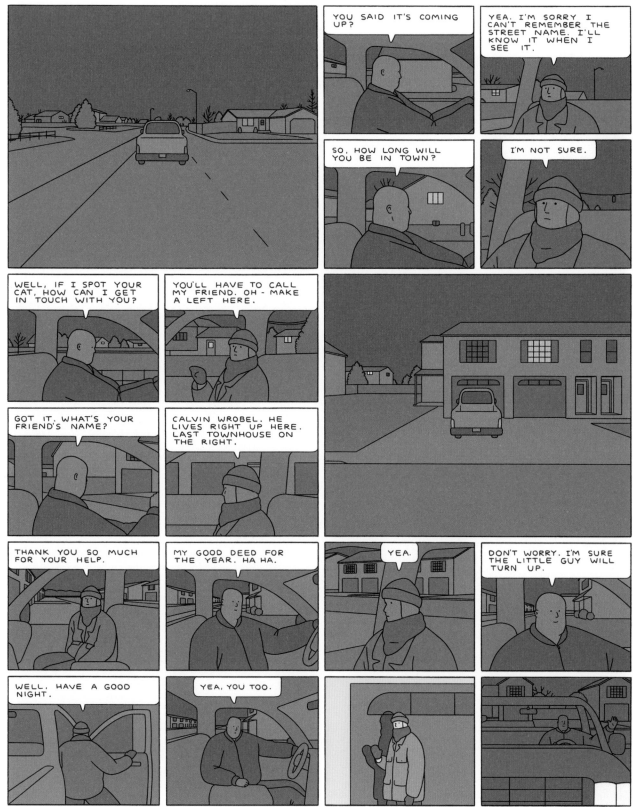

171

HAVE NOT FORGOTTEN

Jason Richmond   11:35 PM
to me

Calvin Wrobel:

Do I need to introduce my-self again? I have been waiting patiently for you to step out of the shadows, but it's clear you have no intention of doing so.

After those 30 kids died, I thought, "OK. Calvin won't sit back and allow this to continue. Any day, he will do the right thing and come forward."

So where are you?

You must have some useful inside knowledge, right? From the Sabrina thing? Just give us a fucking name! This really isn't funny anymore. What kind of monster stands by while children are murdered?

The rest of the world may have forgotten about you, but not me.

A lot of guys only dig into a subject until something new comes along, then they move on to the next big story.

I prefer the more obscure players, people like you, who are on the periphery. Maybe you weren't directly involved, but you can certainly help us uncover who is responsible and bring them to justice.

I just want to help people. Something is clearly out of sorts, can we at least agree on that? You've probably been abused into submission, and my heart goes out to you. These people are so evil, Calvin. I don't think you understand...

Something has to be done. We need you on our side, brother. There is a dark heart at the center of the organization, and I worry that you're getting too close. Set yourself free before it's too late.

What secrets are you hiding? Will you ever blow the whistle? Did they insert a poison capsule into your body that will release if you speak out, or are you just a spineless stooge?

Sometimes I can't believe I'm writing to you, the man whose picture I have analyzed and stared at for days at a time. Do you read this? Will you ever respond to me?

It's just a feeling, but I'm starting to think you are not a good person. No disrespect. Maybe someday you will wake up and do what's right, but until then, you are my sworn enemy.

Give Sabrina my best, you bastard. Let her go. I know you know where she is.

I won't wait for another tragedy to warn you again.

I hate you so much!!!

Always and forever watching you,

Truth Warrior

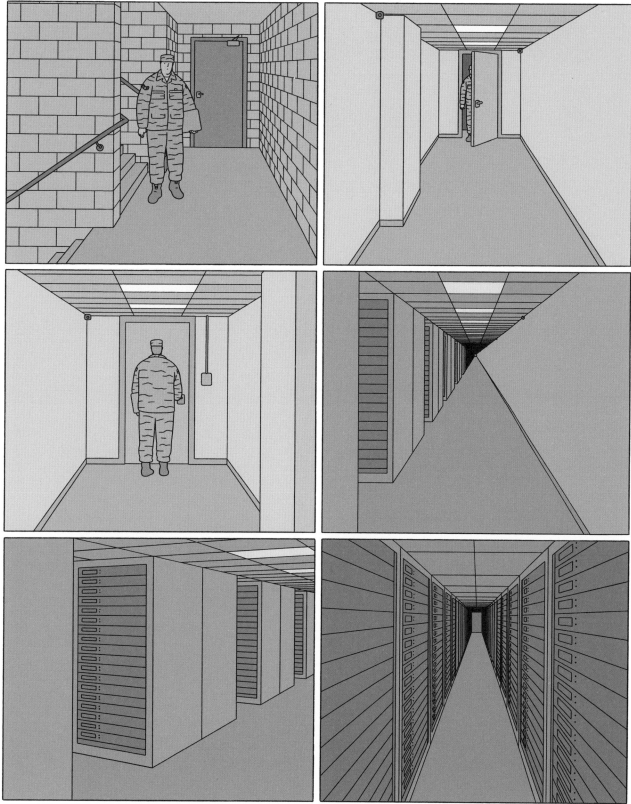

183

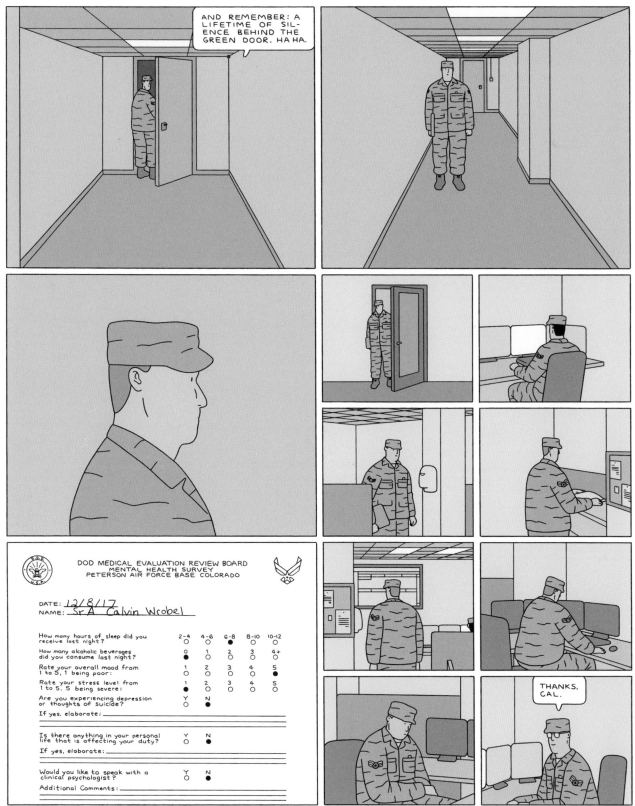

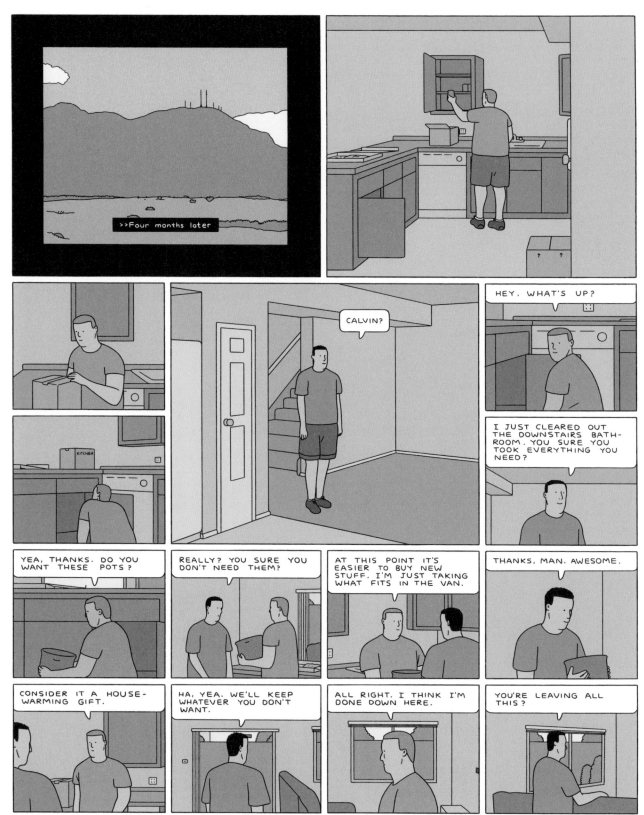

189

193

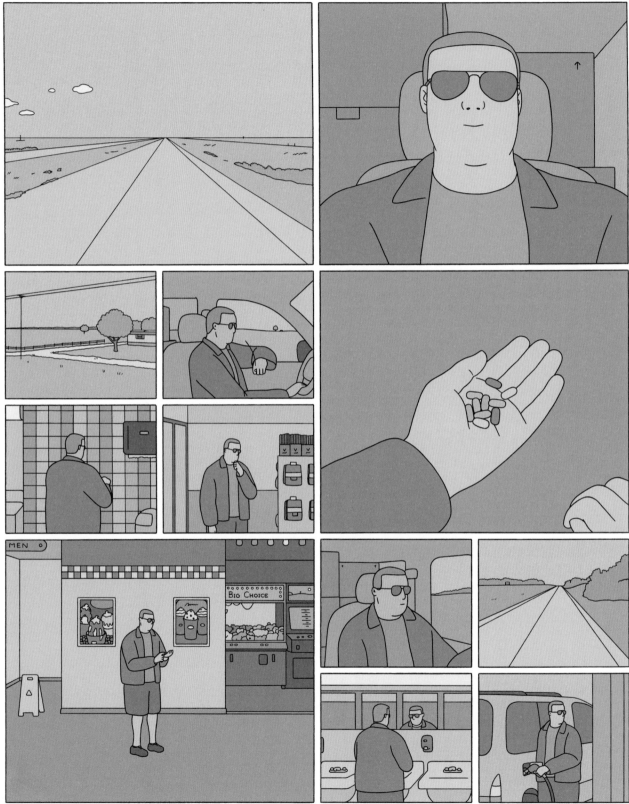

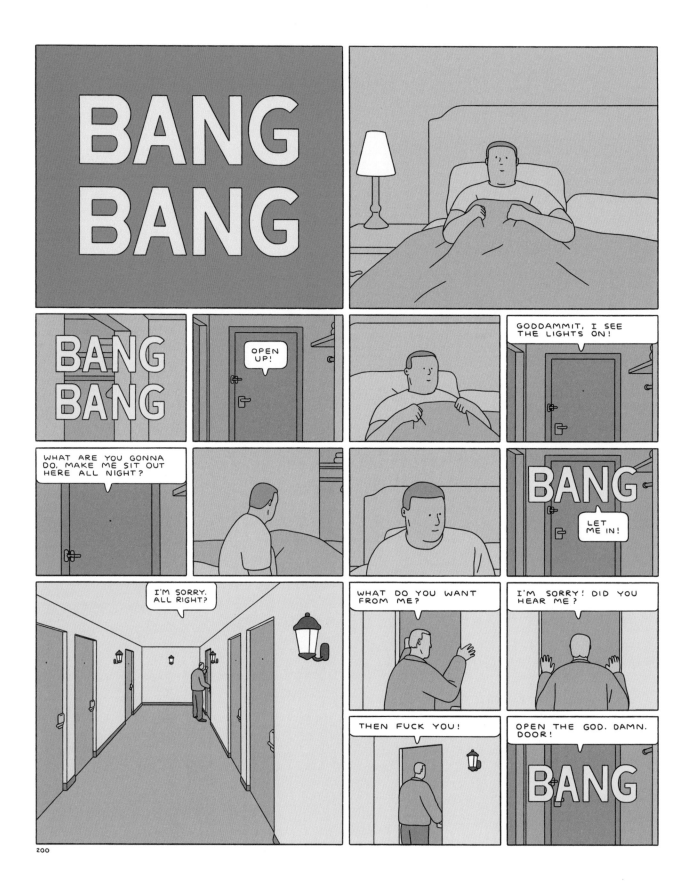

201

NICK DRNASO WAS BORN IN 1989 AND GREW
UP IN PALOS HILLS, ILLINOIS. HIS FIRST
BOOK, BEVERLY, RECEIVED THE LA TIMES
BOOK PRIZE FOR BEST GRAPHIC NOVEL. HE
LIVES IN CHICAGO WITH HIS WIFE AND
THEIR THREE CATS.

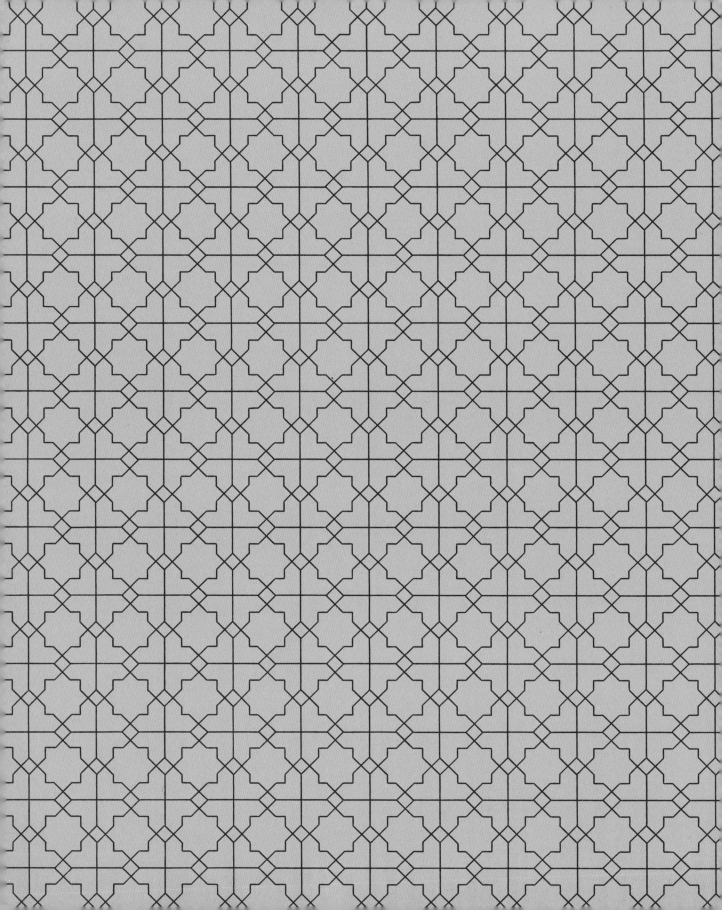